Patrick Harnish

The Adversary

A novel

Jacket design by Erin Gray

Interior Art by Anthony Carrera

Beta reading and editing services by Mac Macabre and Destyn Hehr

Published in the United States by Patrick Harnish and Bookbaby

Published in association with Harnish Music

www.harnishmusic.rocks

Trigger Warning:

This novel has content that is graphic in nature. If you have triggers related to adult language, violence, or sexual violence, you should STOP now. Do not read this novel. Any offensive statements made by the author, are in the context of the character's voice and do not reflect the opinions of the author.

For my Uncle Jerry,

thank you for sharing such a wonderful memory.

A Note From The Author

Journey with me, if you will, into the wild west. Or at least, some version of the wild west.

Through the works of legendary authors like Stephen King, or Hollywood cinema franchises like The Avengers, we've all become familiar with the concepts of shared universes, parallel dimensions, and alternate realities. I won't deny, nor would I want to, that I've borrowed some of those concepts in my own writing. I think you'll find the world contained within these pages is familiar, but not quite right. Something like putting on a favorite coat, then realizing the breast pocket is on a different side than you remembered.

Creating a universe where history and facts aren't set in stone, makes painstaking research mostly unnecessary. Some will say that's just the author being lazy. I won't deny this either. For the most part, I just want to write. Placing my characters into a world similar to ours, but not ours, gives me the freedom to just make things up. Less fact checking. More making shit up. That's my style.

One bit of warning though: My universe, however you want to describe it, is a cruel one. It is not devoid of love, or hope, but its residents endure some pretty fucked up things. And that means you, brave reader, will have to endure them as well. But something tells me you've got the stomach for it.

Above and beyond all else, my desire is for you to enjoy the characters, places, and story you are about to visit. I want you to stay up well past your bedtime, cuddled up in a warm blanket, frantically turning the pages. I want you to anxiously follow along with John Robinson as he pursues a mysterious and terrifying adversary.

Godspeed,

Patrick Harnish

"Gon' head on up to Kansas City

Kansas City is where I run.

Will you come with me to Kansas City?

I hear the girls in that town are lots of fun.

All the girls in Kansas City, know I'm coming, don't they son?."

- Unknown

Prologue

1

Posted in the US Custom House and Post Office, Kansas City, Missouri.

*** WANTED ***

DEAD OR ALIVE

WESLEY NELSON

AKA The Missouri Mauler

AKA The Babyface Killer

$1000 REWARD

6' 1" Tall

175 Lbs.

Red Hair, Fair Complexion

Brown Eyes

Carpenter By Trade

Wanted for murder and rape in Missouri, Kansas, Oklahoma, and Arkansas. Has killed men, women, and children ranging in age from 5 to 61. Is known to impersonate law men and other professions to gain close proximity to victims. Will be armed and dangerous. Has committed murder by use of firearm, knife, and strangulation. Immediately contact the nearest US Marshal's office with information, living prisoner, or proof of execution. June 6, 1898.

2

An excerpt from...

Tales of True Crime

Published 1997

Chapter 9

Serial Killers of the Wild West

Page 148, Entry Wesley Nelson

Serial Killer Wesley Nelson, also known as the Missouri Mauler, or the Babyface Killer, was active from 1879 to the time of his death in 1898. While the details of Wesley's demise are somewhat unclear, it is generally accepted he was killed by his final victim with the aid of an unnamed bounty hunter.

Wesley Nelson is believed to have killed his first victim at the age of nine. Five-year-old Sadie Castle lived five units down from Wesley, and several witnesses reported the two children playing together on March 4th, 1879. This was just hours before she went missing. Sadie was found naked, savagely beaten, and strangled behind their apartment complex later that night. Wesley was interviewed by authorities, but cleared of involvement given his young age. Wesley would not kill again until the age of eighteen.

When he was sixteen, Wesley dropped out of school and took up learning carpentry in Kansas City, Missouri. His father was supportive of Wesley learning a trade, but he would not accept Wesley's refusal to get a proper education. He insisted Wesley improve his ability to read and write or he would no longer be welcome in the family home. His father asked Sarah Vanoy, a sixty-one-year-old retired schoolteacher, to tutor the boy in the evenings. Wesley agreed and diligently attended her tutoring sessions until he was seventeen years old and had proven his ability to read and write proficiently. Sarah told his father that Wesley was a natural student and gifted in the English language; now that he'd decided to apply himself to learning. Wesley also became good friends with Sarah's son, name unknown, and would frequently socialize with the boy until leaving Kansas City at eighteen.

In the early morning of April 15th, 1888, Wesley gained entry to Sarah's small, two-bedroom home in Eastern Kansas City. Sarah was widowed, but her son still lived at the home. However, at the time, he had already reported to work for the day at a nearby factory. Wesley quietly retrieved a pistol from her son's bedroom, then awakened Sarah at gunpoint. It is unknown what conversation they had, but based on other victim accounts, he likely told her his intention was to steal money and leave town.

Wesley had cut the clothesline from Sarah's backyard and utilized the cord to restrain her to her bed. Each limb was secured to a bedpost, with the cords wrapped under the bed frame. Sarah's clothes were cut off her body and she was then brutally raped and tortured over a period of several hours. Wesley stabbed Sarah multiple times during intercourse, but the wounds were shallow and not life-threatening.

Sarah was then cut loose and taken to the cellar, where she was shot, execution-style, in the back of the head. Wesley shot her two more times in the face before positioning her corpse on all fours and inserting the pistol into her vagina. Staging, or posing the

9

victims, was a signature Wesley would continue throughout his gruesome career.

Having known the victim, and seen in the area before the murder, Wesley was questioned about Sarah's death. There was likely some suspicion over Wesley's involvement, but he was ultimately dismissed as a suspect. Several months after Sarah's murder, Wesley left Kansas City and traveled through the Midwest looking for work as a carpenter.

Over the next several years, Wesley would gain employment in various towns and immediately make a good impression with his skill and work ethic. But over time, his odd behavior would cause friction with both his employers and customers. Inevitably, Wesley would commit a murder closely connected to his known associations, and he would leave town. By 1892, Wesley was wanted for multiple murders and a bounty was placed on his head. At its peak, the bounty never surpassed $1000, which was relatively small for a killer of multiple victims.

By the time of his death in 1898, Wesley was believed to have committed fourteen murders, nine rapes, and countless burglaries. It was also in 1898 that Wesley selected his final victim. While working in Fateville, Arkansas at Colton Furniture, Wesley became obsessed with Susan Colton, wife of proprietor Henry Colton. Susan would run the front office of Colton's Furniture and often acted as an indirect supervisor to the hired hands working in the store. Although he was a skilled carpenter, Wesley was only hired to deliver furniture to customers. He often resented this, harboring anger towards Henry. Other employees recounted how Wesley often talked about Henry and how he was unworthy of Susan. He would go on to say that if Henry ever hurt Susan, Wesley would make him pay. His co-workers attributed this to his odd behavior.

But on September 6th, 1898, Wesley unexpectedly showed up at the Colton residence. It was nearly sundown when Henry discovered Wesley crouched behind the bushes in his front yard. Having been asked for an explanation, Wesley claimed another worker was angry with Henry and was coming to his house to shoot him. Wesley, concerned for the Colton family's safety, immediately came to the Colton Residence and was trying to locate the potential gunman. He told Henry that he should retrieve his rifle and help search the property. When Henry turned, Wesley struck him on the back of the head with a small wooden club he had concealed in a leather satchel. This satchel accompanied Wesley to many of his crimes, and it is said he referred to it as his "hit kit" (a phrase later adopted by another mid-western serial killer, named Dennis Rader, also known as the BTK).

The two men entered the home, scuffling as Wesley tried to subdue Henry further. He was eventually knocked unconscious, at which point Wesley forced Susan to reveal where Henry kept his pistol. He assured her his only concern was money and leaving town, but he needed time to think, and wanted a gun to keep things under control. Believing Wesley's story, she complied and helped him retrieve Henry's sidearm. Henry eventually regained consciousness, and both he and Susan were led into the cellar at gunpoint. Susan was forced to tie Henry to a wooden beam with a rope that Wesley carried in his leather satchel.

After ensuring Henry was secured to the cellar beam, Wesley escorted Susan back upstairs and tied her to the bedposts. He maintained his intention was to obtain money and leave town, and frequently went back and forth from Susan to Henry as well as pilfering through the contents of their home.

On his final trip down to the cellar, Wesley revealed a large knife taken from the Colton's kitchen. He taunted Henry for several minutes, calmly describing his sexual intentions with Susan. And then, without warning, he plunged the kitchen knife into Henry's chest. Wesley then proceeded upstairs where he revealed his true intentions to Susan and began his slow and tortuous ritual of rape.

11

Unknown to Wesley, Henry was still alive. The knife had missed his heart and vital arteries, and his bindings had become loose enough to free himself. Fortunately, Henry had also been working on a rifle in the cellar. It was in working condition, but only had one bullet in the chamber. Despite being beaten unconscious and stabbed, Henry was able to find the strength to pull himself upstairs and confront Wesley.

In another unusual turn of events, an unknown bounty hunter was investigating a tip that Wesley Nelson, AKA the Missouri Mauler, might be working at a local furniture store under the name Weston Harper. The bounty hunter was paying a visit to the owner of said furniture store to ask questions about the employee, Weston. He opted to visit the owner's residence, as opposed to the furniture store, so as not to alert Wesley. When arriving at the residence of Henry Colton, the bounty hunter heard several gunshots and entered the home.

Henry Colton, still alive and determined to save his wife, had found Wesley naked, looming over Susan, holding a pistol. Henry called out to Wesley and fired, striking him in the shoulder and sending him reeling against the wall. But Wesley also fired his pistol, fatally striking Henry in the head.

Susan began screaming hysterically, prompting Wesley to club her with the butt of his pistol. It was at this moment the bounty hunter entered the room and took aim at the assailant. However, the bounty hunter's pistol jammed and he was also shot in the head by Wesley. Yet the wound did not prove fatal. Disoriented and in pain, the bounty hunter fell to the ground and dropped his firearm. Wesley, surprised by both rescue attempts, quickly fled the home, still naked, with only his gun in hand.

Shortly after, the bounty hunter came to. He checked Henry Colton for a pulse and determined he was deceased. He pulled the large kitchen knife from the man's chest and cut Susan's bindings. He then left the house in pursuit of Wesley. But perhaps still disoriented, he did not retrieve his firearm. The facts of what happened next are the subject of much debate, but the best evidence suggests that Susan retrieved the bounty hunter's pistol and followed both men out. She caught up to them and just before Wesley was about to shoot the bounty hunter again, she killed Wesley with a single shot to the head.

Most unusual of all was that Wesley's body was never recovered. Many have speculated as to what happened, but by all accounts, it was gone before lawmen arrived. Despite the lack of a corpse, the reputation of both Susan Colton and the unknown bounty hunter compelled the US Marshall's Office to award the bounty split two ways. It is said the bounty hunter gave his half to Susan Colton, who was now a widow. Although there is speculation to this day, it is widely agreed that Wesley Nelson was killed in this encounter and no further murders were ever attributed to him. Despite Wesley's horrific crimes and double-digit body count, he is best known for being a serial killer who was killed by one of his victims.

Part One

The Tragedies That Shape Us

"I have no restraint

I have no fear

I keep death at my side

I hold it so dear

I have no remorse

I have no fear

I keep death at my side

I keep it so near." HARNISH, The Adversary

1

Last Night, It Was a Reaper

Last night, it was a reaper. The embodiment of death. Its tattered black robe whipped in the warm August wind. A black hood surrounded what should have been a face. *Or a skull.* But there was neither. Only a deep void of black.

John, at five feet and eleven inches, stood frozen and stared up at the creature. It was easily seven feet tall. The handle of its sickle planted into the ground like a wizard's staff. A curved blade arced above its head and spit out shimmers of moonlight.

John had no intention of fleeing from the creature. But what did he intend to do? The same as every time before, he felt paralyzed with fear. But other emotions were boiling up inside him. Rage was closest to the surface. It wailed at the fear and sent electric bolts through his arms and legs. *Move John. Destroy it!*

How does one do such a thing? Bring death to Death? It was certainly a hopeless endeavor, but still a righteous one. Hadn't this monster taken everything? Even if John were to die, isn't trying to kill it the only thing worth living for?

A scream was working its way up from John's belly, like lava rushing to escape the Earth in a fiery explosion. No, not a scream. *A battle cry.* It erupted from John's mouth. *Aaaaaarrrrrrrrrrr!* There was a gun in his hand, and he raised it at this angel of death. The creature's eyes caught fire inside the deep black of its hood. They glowed like hot coals, giving glimpses of the foul thing's skull. The gun in his hand suddenly grew hot. The metal barrel turned into molten goo, and he dropped it onto the ground. It burned in a pile at his feet. Desperate, his hands thrust upwards in an attempt to grab the reaper's neck.

John could sense the sickle moving at supernatural speed, slicing through the air. In those milliseconds of time, he was able to wonder if his impending death would hurt. To wonder if his head, lopped off and falling to the ground, would still see as it fell? In his heart, he mostly expected instant darkness. The same never-ending blackness of the reaper's face.

But instead, John felt a tickle on his cheek. Something was buzzing around him and brushed against his face. Small flakes of snow landed on his lips and melted. He opened his eyes and then immediately squinted at the flood of daylight. Blackness, this was not. A buzzing insect made another pass at John's face, and he swatted it away. Was it a fly, or possibly a bee?

"Too damn cold for bugs," he complained in a raspy voice.

His head ached. It ached from yesterday's overindulgence of whiskey. It ached from the dream. The goddamn recurring nightmare that John seemed doomed to have for the rest of his life. This time it was a reaper. True, it had never been that before. But it was always some type of monster. A stand-in beast, filling in for the creature's true form. He could remember every blood-soaked detail of that night. He just couldn't remember what spilled all the blood.

2

Dead Brothers and Brain Tumors

"You've been asleep for two days, ya' know that?" remarked John's brother Jerry. Deceased now for twenty-five years, Jerry looked as alive as ever. He lay on his back with his hands behind his head. As kids, their beds were side by side and that's always how Jerry preferred to lay. He would look up at the ceiling and ramble to John for all hours of the night. And now, here he was again, still twelve years old, lying next to John's campfire.

John was lying on his side and still squinting from the sudden brightness. Yet that was Jerry alright. He could see and hear him as clear as day.

"You're not real. I'm not still dreaming, I know that. But you're not real," John muttered.

Jerry turned to look at John with a smug sneer. He felt around the ground next to him until he found a good size pebble. He hurled it across the camp, hitting John in the face. "That feel real?"

John, head throbbing and face now stinging, felt a pang of anger. Then suddenly nostalgic. This definitely wasn't real, but

17

delusion or not, it was nice to see his little brother "I missed you, butthole." John smiled and burst into laughter.

"I missed you too, dickhead." Jerry flashed a crooked grin John hadn't seen in over two decades.

In an already strange world, things were even stranger lately. John had been seeing things. Shadows and shapes in the corner of his eye. Figures and people far ahead of him on the road. People that always seemed to fade as he got closer. *Mirages*, he had told himself. And there were also smells. For the last week, John kept catching the distinct smell of oranges. He had only encountered the citrus scent a handful of times in his life. Mainly as a kid, when Cal Piglee would get a shipment in at his general store. It was a wonderful smell. And now here it was again, on the brisk November wind, in the middle of Nowhere, Oklahoma.

"What's wrong with me?" John asked.

"In the future, they'll call it glioblastoma." Jerry seemed sullen now.

"Gly-Ooo-Blaztoma?"

Jerry scrunched his face and paused in thought. "Remember Uncle Ricky, and how he got that big lump in his neck? And it kept getting bigger and bigger and then he got sicker and sicker until he died?"

"Yes?"

"It's like you've got one of those, but it's on your brain. Brain cancer. Glioblastoma. Bad shit."

"I'm dying?"

"Yes. You've had it a long time now. But it was kind of, I don't know. Sleeping. Now it's awake and its tentacles are moving down through your brain. Making you see things. Smell things. Giving you headaches and making you sleep for days on end."

"Is that why I'm seeing you? Are you a ghost or a hallucination?"

"A little bit of both, maybe. Who knows? But that's not what's important." Jerry's tone turned to impatience.

"It seems pretty fucking important."

"It's going to kill you, but it also protects you... from him." Jerry turned on his side to face John. Small tendrils of smoke were coming up from a nearly dead campfire that burned between them. The coals gave off just enough heat to give Jerry's face a wavy quality.

"I don't want protection from him. I want to find him." John felt his heart beat faster. His clenched fists started to shake. "I want to wrap my hands around his neck and squeeze until his eyes pop out of his head." There was a short pause, then John felt the anger subside and he dropped his eyes. "But I don't even know what it is. Is it even a *him*?"

"It's definitely a *him*." Jerry paused briefly, considering his next words. "That thing in your head doesn't just protect you from his power. It doesn't just blind him from seeing inside your mind. It draws you to him. Brings you close. You must know that by now. But your time is running out, John. "

"Getting close to him isn't fucking good enough! I'm always too late! Just like I was with my family. I'm there in time to see his carnage." John's voice was getting louder. "I'm never there to stop it."

"Then quit drinking so much. Quit sleeping so much. Move quicker. Think quicker. Follow the lights."

"If you can tell me all this, just tell me where he is! Tell me where to go. Tell me how I stop him."

"There are rules, big bubba. I can't do that. Now get moving."

And just like that, twelve-year-old Jerry was gone again. With a groan, John pulled himself into a sitting position and rubbed his eyes. Had he really slept for two days? Had he stirred enough to keep the fire going? It was down to coals now, but it surely would have burned out had he slept for that long. Or did his dead little brother stoke the fire for him too? Ghost or delusion, Jerry was right. It was time to get moving. There was a monster to kill.

3

Deconstruction

Some things are timeless. Having a drink at the bar, for example. Or in this case, the saloon. It was 1902 in Harrison, Kansas, and this particular saloon didn't have a name. It was just, *the saloon*. When you are the only watering hole in town, that works out okay.

The saloon had all the cliche charm you might expect from a wild west establishment. Two large swinging doors served as the main entrance. In one corner, a black iron stove stood ready to warm the saloon's patrons. But it was still August, and a hot August at that. The stove wouldn't be back in action for another two months. In another corner was a rather nice piano. It wasn't large, but looked well-cared for. While everything in the saloon, from the plank floorboards to the dozen or so table and chair sets, had a nice coating of dust, the piano did not. Its polished wooden frame stood out, almost gleamed, against the other furnishings. There was no

20

piano player right now, mind you. This was a Wednesday night, and business was slow.

Charlie Sandusky, the saloon's proprietor and bartender, was serving two customers. John Robinson sat at the bar's end with Dodd Stevens. To look at them, you saw two men on opposite ends of the spectrum.

John was a rather handsome fellow. His hair was short and dark. Perfectly combed and parted. His features were sharp, but there was a smooth quality to his face. He was so clean-shaven you might think he had exited Ross Whitman's barbershop, exactly one building north, before entering the saloon. John's clothes were simple and professional. Black slacks, a white button-up shirt, and a thin black jacket. His black leather shoes shined with the same luster of his perfectly parted dark hair. If not for a loosened collar, John looked as though he could still be at work. That being at the Robinson Bank and Trust, exactly three blocks south and next to the sheriff's office. Yes, John was the *Robinson*, in *Robinson Bank and Trust*.

Dodd, on the other hand, was not a handsome fellow. His hair and clothes were unkempt. You could barely see his face through a wild ginger beard. His eyes seemed to be set too close together. His mother, a heavy drinker, had given Dodd the gift of fetal alcohol syndrome. You can file that away with Glioblastomas for now. Folks around this time would just say Dodd was feeble-minded.

Dodd was the proprietor of nothing. I guess you might call him the town's handyman. He bounced from odd job to odd job and had a good reputation for his hard work and craftsmanship. If the work involved mechanical knowledge, or carpentry skills, Dodd wasn't feeble-minded at all. But he was also the town drunk; a functional alcoholic if there ever was one. When work was good, he'd tie one on nightly at the saloon. By sunrise, he'd be repairing a barn or replacing someone's busted wagon wheel. On a night such

21

as this, it didn't matter if work had been good. John had a soft spot for old Dodd and would keep the whiskey flowing, free of charge. After all, John knew the minuscule amount of savings Dodd held in his bank account.

"Lights! Like giant candles floating in the sky. I've seen 'em the past three nights. Sometimes out over Keegan's farm. Sometimes out in the south woods," Dodd remarked with drunken enthusiasm. He looked from John to Charlie and back again to John. "Well...you believe me?"

"I believe...you...are drunk." John grinned.

Dodd scowled, then turned to Charlie. "And you?"

"I believe...you...are...both drunk." Charlie also grinned as he polished a glass behind the bar.

"Yes. Tis true. I am drunk." Dodd humorously raised his hands in a guilty exclamation. "However, what I saw was real and it was prior to drinking this piss you sell us as whiskey." Dodd tipped back his fifth shot of the night.

"You seem oddly fond of drinking my piss," Charlie countered. And after a short pause, all three of them burst into laughter.

"Look, look, Dodd. I believe you. You've been seeing weird lights in the sky. But what do you think it is you are seeing?" John said, regaining his composure.

"Not natural. Know that. Spirits I think."

"Spirits, eh?"

"Yeah, spirits. I've heard of it happening before. Just never seen it. Till now."

"Might be, Dodd. To the spirits, then. Charlie, fill us back up."

22

John and Dodd gave their newly refreshed glasses a light toast and tipped back their sixth shots of the night.

At this point in time, John still possessed some control over his alcoholism. He had a weakness for drinking, but he kept it in check. At home, John had his beautiful wife, Sascha. They were crazy about each other. He had two precious nine-year-old daughters, identical twins. Sarah Marie, and Mary Ellen. He adored them. Robinson Bank and Trust had started as a small operation in Harrison, but had now branched out to Chanoot, Iolta, and Coffey. John was the richest man in town, and quickly becoming one of the richest men in the state of Kansas. Simply put, there just wasn't a lot he needed to drown in booze.

Funny thing about booze though, it doesn't really need a reason. And on several occasions, it had certainly gotten the better of John. He wasn't a mean drunk, at least not to Sascha. And he wasn't a cheating drunk, but there was a two-year period it certainly took a toll on his marriage. In John's mind, drinking was like slowly walking towards the edge of a cliff. If he walked just far enough, the view was incredible. But a step or two further and it was a freefall. Tonight, after tipping back his sixth shot, the view was great, and he knew it was time to turn back.

John pushed out the double doors of the saloon and was instantly met with a steady breeze. The temperature had cooled down from the day, but there was still a hint of heat on the wind. And a scent. *Oranges?* He slowly walked over to his spotted palomino horse, Carl. The whiskey was definitely hitting him now. The world seemed slightly off its axis.

"Can you get this drunken young man home, Carl?" John affectionately stroked the horse's mane. "What do you mean I'm not young anymore? You're not so young yourself." John giggled childishly and looked around. The Glioblastoma was present at this time, but he had no delusions about the horse talking back. He was just drunk. "You're an asshole sometimes, Carl," he said in a lowered voice as he released Carl's ties. John gripped the saddle horn and placed his left foot into the stirrup. He steadied himself with a deep breath, then swiftly lifted himself onto the horse. They rode into the hot wind and began the short trek home.

At a slow drunken pace, the saloon to home on horseback was about a ten-minute ride. John was ahead of that pace when he met the dirt trail leading up to his house. He had found the jaunt home sobering. It was windy, but otherwise a beautiful night. He

paused for a moment to take it all in. He looked back at the town. Not a candlelight burned that he could see. The town looked small under the moonlight, but in his mind's eye, he saw more.

He could imagine the silhouettes of buildings expanding out for miles in all directions. He could imagine those same buildings climbing increasingly higher into the night sky. On a business trip to Kansas City, he had seen lights that glow with no flame, just electricity. And now he saw those lights lining the streets of Harrison. In Kansas City, there was talk of horseless wagons and other wonders on the horizon. It would all be here. The town didn't look small; it looked humble. "She's really gonna get big, Carl."

From the corner of his eye, something gleamed. He turned back towards his house and in the distance, a shooting star burned as it descended to earth. There was no sound. Just a fiery green arrow plummeting from the heavens. Living in the early American West - a time not polluted by electric lights - a man saw many shooting stars. But this was one of the closest John had ever witnessed.

"It's beautiful, Carl." And with those words, the last of its flames extinguished and disappeared "That spirit is at rest now, boy. Let's get on up to the house and get some rest ourselves. Tomorrow we'll tell Dodd we saw one of his lights." John glanced down at Carl. "What? It's not a lie, just stretching the truth a little. Besides, it will make him feel good. Like he's not crazy." Carl approved, or so John told himself, and they began to move up the dirt path.

Suddenly, without explanation, John became overwhelmed with dread. The shooting star, which had filled him with wonder moments ago, now felt more like an ill omen. It was like eating something delicious, only for it to leave a rotten aftertaste in your mouth. John's arms broke out in gooseflesh. And even with the hot August wind, John felt a chill come over his body. His house, much like the town, had not a single candlelight burning. That was not like Sascha. No matter how late he would sometimes stay out at the

25

saloon, she would always leave a candle burning for him at home. It was the dimmest of red flags, but John knew something was terribly wrong.

He clicked his tongue twice, and Carl shot into a full run. At that moment, Carl and John, horse and man, were as connected as they'd ever been. They could feel the nervousness in each other and the danger all around them. John's hand dropped to his side and found the comforting grip of his revolver. Working at a bank in the wild west, and visiting places simply known as the saloon, a man was wise to get comfortable with a firearm. John certainly was, but he knew he was riding into something he wasn't prepared for.

He pulled back on Carl's reigns as they approached the front steps of his home. The horse was so keyed up, for a moment, John thought he may not stop in time. But Carl stopped on a dime and John dismounted just as quickly. There was no horse tie in the front of the house. John gave Carl two swats on the rear. "Go on. To the barn."

The pasture gate was open, and Carl wasn't one to wander off. He rarely understood any of John's drunken conversation, but this command he grasped completely and raced into the field. Carl had a built-in alarm going back thousands of genetic years. There was a predator close. Something like a rattlesnake. Something like a wolf. Something like every creature that had ever preyed on a horse. Carl was worried for his master, but also eager to put distance between himself and the unknown threat.

John ascended his porch steps. With escalating terror, he could see the front door was standing wide open. Again, he felt for the grip of his revolver. His hand made purchase with the gun and he slid it out from the holster.

It was a beautiful piece. Dodd had crafted it by hand and gifted it to John the previous year. John assumed some of the metal had been repurposed from another piece. But even so, Dodd had taken great care to refurbish and polish the frame, barrel, and cylinder. As for the action, it was Dodd's finest woodwork. Etched into the finished white oak handle, with a precise arch, Dodd had inscribed R - O - B - I - N - S - O - N.

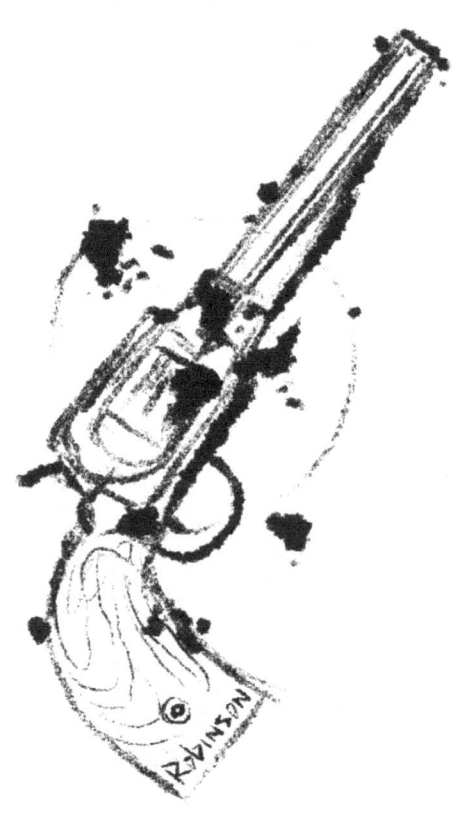

John cherished the gift from his friend. With it, he had shot a good number of bottles and cans. It had scared away coyotes from the property. It had even scared away a would-be bank robber or two, just by being visible on John's hip. Tonight, he hoped it would be enough to deal with the threat inside his home.

John walked softly across his porch and into the waiting darkness. He paused inside the door. He listened closely and allowed his eyes a few moments to adjust. His pupils expanded and drank up the moonlight coming in through the windows. Nothing looked out of place in the foyer. But there were no signs of his family. And there was no sound coming from anywhere in the home.

John felt in his breast pocket and pulled out a wooden box of matches. He knelt beside the small oil lamp next to the door and cautiously placed his gun beside it. His hands were shaking, but he struck the match and ignited the cotton wick of the lamp. He rose to his feet. With the lamp on his left side and the outstretched gun on his right, he began to explore the house.

John didn't have to get far before the horror of this night would be revealed. Turning into his living room, he saw something that might as well have been branded into his brain with a hot iron.

The room was centered by a fireplace on the back wall, with two oak rocking chairs on either side. It was Sarah Marie and Mary Ellen's favorite place to sit. On cool nights, they would beg John to make them a fire. They'd ask him to rock them and fight over who he would rock first. Ultimately, they would both end up in his lap, all crammed into one chair. With every passing year, they seemed to get a foot taller, and it was getting harder and harder to do.

John looked over these memories, felt them, experienced them all at once. But they couldn't displace the gruesome reality before him. The limbless, naked body of each child was seated in the opposing chairs. John, who could most easily distinguish the twins from their eyes, saw their eyes had been removed from their sockets. Blood dripped down from the empty black holes. It appeared as though they were crying tears of blood. With a pang of sickening guilt, John realized he couldn't tell the two girls apart.

In the open firebox, and stacked on the grate, were parts of his daughters. Their severed limbs were neatly arranged like firewood. Through the cords of flesh, he could make out some of their small fingers and one bloody knee. Jutting out over the hearth, he could see one of his daughter's feet, missing all but two of its toes.

The urge to vomit felt overwhelming. But what came out of John wasn't puke. It was more of a guttural howl. It was the sound of pure, all-consuming grief. *Waaaaaaaaah!* John's eyes welled up with tears, and a long strand of spit dripped from his bottom lip. He was disoriented and in anguish, but still thinking. Processing.

Whoever did this never intended to burn his daughter's limbs in the fire. They wanted this to be seen. This was someone's hellish artwork, left for John to view. How would someone know this was a special place to him and his daughters? That didn't seem possible. But this was too personal to be random madness.

It's never too warm for a fire.

Something spoke to John from behind. He turned quickly, strings of saliva still dangling from his mouth. He raised the gun, but saw nothing. Had he heard a voice? Or felt it? It was more like a thought in his mind, but not his own.

You're hard to see inside, that's rare. But I can see enough.

"Who are you?" John screamed.

You liked to rock them together in one chair, but they were getting too big. The sun will rise. The sun will set. How fast go by these days.

29

Words were exploding in John's mind like fireworks. *POP! POP! POP!*

I bet you can fit them both on your lap now. If you can keep them from sliding off, that is. Ha. Ha. Ha.

The voice, which wasn't a voice, was actually chuckling. And all at once, John felt consumed. By nothing. By everything. He felt like he was floating in the middle of the ocean, being toyed with by a shark. What was this thing? This man? It wasn't a shark, but it had a shark's voice, didn't it? It had a shark's thoughts. Desperate and scared, John squeezed the trigger and fired a shot into the front wall of his house.

A scuttering noise went through the foyer and he heard footsteps climbing the stairs to the second floor. He followed in pursuit. He could not see what it was, but he could feel something was there. It moved swiftly up the stairs and into John and Sascha's bedroom. John had the distinct impression he wasn't giving chase, but rather being led. It seemed foolish to follow, but there was no time to reconsider. Whatever horror lay ahead would have to be faced. Like cattle, he moved through the chute and entered what would certainly be his death room.

It was a death room indeed, but not his own. He had been brought here to *witness*.

In the 20th century, much would be learned about the psychology of killers. Serial killers, to be more precise, would have specific terminology to explain their behavior. This scene, illuminated by John's dim oil lamp, could only be categorized as frenzied overkill. The killer would be disorganized, in a state of uncontrolled rage and fantasy. If one came upon this site in the woods, one might think Sascha was the victim of an animal attack. There was so much gore, so much dismemberment. It would be difficult to imagine even a pack of wolves had done so much damage.

John, now in his own mental state of unraveling, looked upon the bed where, just the night before, he and Sascha made love. All that remained of Sascha was now in a thousand pieces and parts, splattered across the room. She was a chunky puddle in the middle of the bed and parts of her could be seen oozing down the walls, dangling from the ceiling, and congealing on the floor. John moved forward, and the toe of his right boot slipped on something. He planted his left foot and caught his balance just before tumbling over. He raised his boot and illuminated the underside with lamplight. A bloody, severed nipple slid down his scuffed leather sole and plopped onto the floor. John fell to his knees and began to wretch.

I made her right, John. A woman should be...deconstructed.

John raised his head, and his eyes searched the room for the shark. For the wolf. For the rattlesnake man. "Show yourself!" he demanded through clenched teeth. The taste in his mouth was a mixture of vomit and blood.

Did you know she was pregnant?

John's throat dropped into the bottom of his stomach. He didn't know if he could believe the words of this phantom, but his heart told him it was true. Without speaking a word, he raised his revolver and pointed the barrel at his own temple.

That's right. End it. Go be with them. Is that what you think will happen? Sorry to tell you, John, only darkness waits for you when you pull that trigger. This life is all you have, and I've taken all of it away.

In the corner of his eye, in the corner of his room, he saw...something. It was as though something in the corner was blurry, but slowly coming into focus. In a quick and smooth reaction, John redirected his pistol to the corner and fired three rounds. There was a screeching cry. John could not tell whether it was an audible cry or just within his mind. Either way, it cut through his brain like a razor, and he instinctively covered his ears.

He was still unable to see the creature, but his sense of it was stronger. He could feel it was alarmed and in retreat. Something darted past him and exited the bedroom. Despite the throbbing pain in his head, John saw an opportunity and pursued. It was possible he hurt the creature, and now was his chance to avenge his family.

John raced down the stairs, but dropped the oil lamp as he went. It shattered in a hot explosion, sending bits of glass and oil tumbling down the steps. He navigated through his home's shadows, all the while sensing, feeling, knowing that this thing was only steps ahead of him. He pursued it through their family dining room, into the kitchen, and towards a narrow doorway leading out the back of the house.

When he stepped back out into the hot August air, time seemed to slow. Moonlight poured down and illuminated a killer. John looked ahead and could almost see the thing he pursued. But it was pushing back with all its will. Masking itself. Making itself unseen. What was this thing? It could speak without words, in a voice that sounded like John's own thoughts. It could reach into his memories and pick at them like scabs. It could blind his eyes from its true form.

A rattling noise echoed in his ears. In the distance, he could hear Carl neighing with excitement and fear. John looked down and could see a rattlesnake five feet ahead in the grass. It was curled up, poised, and ready to strike. Even further ahead, towards the back of the pasture, he could see wolves pacing and circling. Their eyes blazed with red fire, and John knew they were moving in on Carl.

"None of this is real." John steadied his thoughts and lifted the revolver. He watched as the barrel moved up, passing over the

32

rattlesnake, and then pointed straight ahead at empty space. "I think you're right there, in front of me."

Then squeeze the trigger, mother fucker.

The phantom voice seemed to take on a slow southern drawl. John's trigger finger trembled. Somewhere in his brain, signals were launching out, traveling through his nervous system, moving through the millions of channels and pathways that connect brain to finger. *Pull. Pull. Pull.* John's entire hand was shaking. Despite his considerable effort, his finger never did pull that trigger. The gun never fired. In fact, it tumbled to the ground. He looked down just in time to see the gargantuan fangs of the rattlesnake lunging towards him.

John opened his eyes, squinting through a flood of daylight. The dream had come again, as it did most nights now. This time, it was a rattlesnake. It had been other things, in other dreams. Many times it had been a werewolf, a vampire, or a reptilian monster, like he used to read about as a kid. Cal Piglee never kept those publications on the sales floor. They were discreetly stashed behind the counter and would set you back about three pennies an issue. The dream monsters John encountered were free, and never-ending.

He was at the start of a long journey. He would travel the terrain of the American Midwest for nearly ten years to come, following something he felt drawn to, but could never quite catch. At times he would see lights in the sky he couldn't explain. He'd call them spirits and think of his old friend Dodd. Near the end of his journey, he'd dream the creature was a reaper. Something it had never been before.

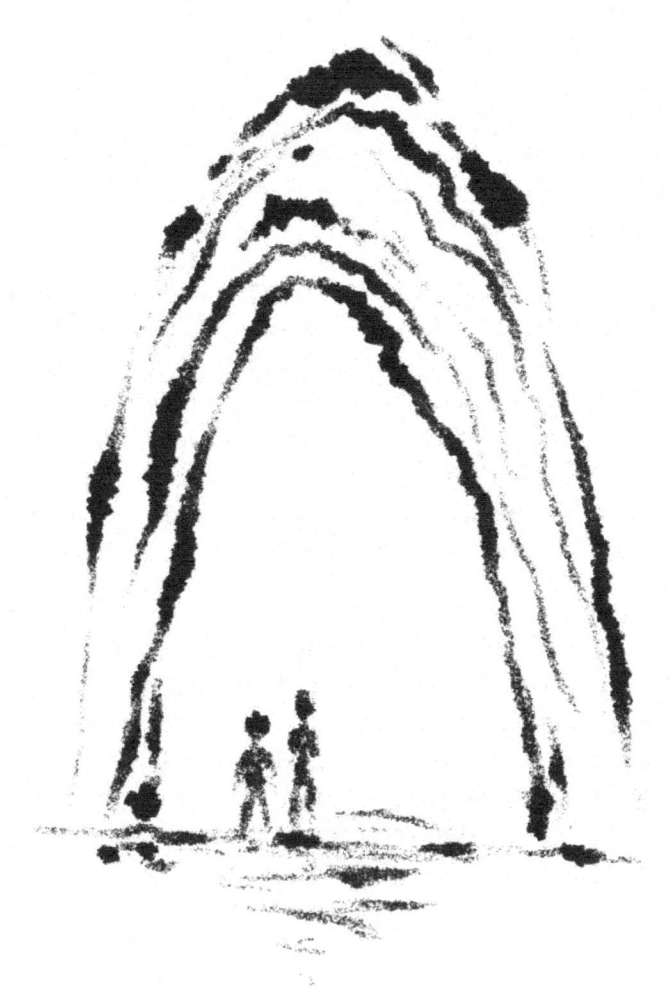

4

Do You Want To See A Cave?

Click. Click. Click. Jerry didn't know what John was doing, but he knew it was goddamn annoying. Jerry was lying on his back, with his interlaced fingers behind his head. He had a lot of things to think about. But how could he concentrate with all that damn clicking? He peered over at his brother, who was sitting at a small wooden desk. There was a cloth sack sitting beside him on the desktop. John would reach in the bag, pull out a penny, closely examine it, then deposit it into a drawer on the other side. The coins would drop into the drawer with a maddening *click*.

It was a small bedroom the two boys shared. After all, it was 1887 and most folks lived in modest conditions. The Robinson family was no different. Their home, which was more of a large cabin, comprised two bedrooms, a cramped cooking and eating area, and a center living space heated by a rusty wood-burning stove. John and Jerry's bedroom was the tightest space of all, and the sound of his brother clicking those pennies into the desk drawer was likely to drive Jerry mad.

"John," Jerry said firmly. No reply.

Click.

"John." Slightly louder this time. No reply.

Click.

"John!"

"What?" John responded robotically.

"What the hell are you doing?"

35

"Huh?" John seemed a thousand miles away. One particular penny had him enthralled.

"I said, what the hell are you doing? I might kill you if you keep clicking those pennies into the desk!"

"Like to see you try, butthole," John said playfully. He was three years older than Jerry, and while the two of them rarely fought, John was the top dog when they did.

"At least tell me what you're doing so I know why I'm going insane."

"You see this?" John turned and held a penny out.

"Yeah. It's a penny. So what?"

"I had two dollars saved up from all the wood I cut in the winter for Mr. Everton. When Pa took me into town yesterday, I went to the bank and exchanged those two dollars for this sack of pennies." John looked at Jerry as though this answered all his questions.

"I'm trying to connect the dots here, but you aren't making it easy."

"Some pennies aren't just pennies. Some are special. For example, it just so happens there was a batch of birch cents printed in 1810 that had a misprint. Come here, come closer." John reached into the sack and retrieved another penny. "Yeah, oh yeah, here we go. Look at this."

Jerry stood up and grabbed the coin. "Alright, what am I looking at?"

"You see around Lady Liberty's head how she's got a bunch of stars? How many you count?"

Jerry took a moment. "Thirteen."

"Right, like the thirteen colonies. Now look at this one." John held out the coin he was previously examining "How many stars?"

Jerry held it close to his face. "Twelve. This one's only got twelve."

"Yup. 1810, birch cent, minting error. And I found one."

"So what's the big deal?"

"The big deal is a coin collector will give me twenty dollars for that baby. Twenty-five dollars maybe."

"Lying ass."

"Nope." John plucked the cent back with a grin.

"Lucky dog dick!"

The two boys laughed heartily, before clasping a hand to their mouths. They didn't have the strictest of parents, but their colorful language did occasionally earn them a whipping.

"I'll go through the rest later. Do you want to see a cave?" John said while placing the prized penny in a small box under his bed. There was a final, albeit quieter, *click*.

"Well, yeah. Where's it at?"

"About two miles away. Maybe three. My friend Nelson, Mr. Everton's boy, he showed it to me back in December. It was too cold to explore, but it's warm enough now. It's on their land, but they said I'm welcome anytime if I don't do no shooting."

"Can you like, go inside it?"

"Oh yeah it's big."

Jerry was starting to get excited. "You've gotta show me. I've never been in a big cave."

"You wanna know something else?"

"What?"

"Nelson told me his grandpa knew some old Spanish outlaws and they hid some gold in the cave. You think that penny is worth something, wait until we find some Spanish treasure."

"This is going to be the best day of my life!" Jerry, not ten minutes ago, was ready to strangle his big brother for incessantly clicking those pennies into their desk drawer. But now he felt nothing but love for him. John was fifteen; three years older than Jerry, but he generally treated him like an equal. He treated him like a friend. He was always ready to take Jerry on boyish adventures. Jerry had a feeling this one might be the best adventure of all. And with that thought, the boys were off to Mr. Everton's cave looking for Spanish treasure.

Jerry, in his short life, was never speechless. But standing at the entrance of the cave, he was about as close as he'd ever been. It was truly picturesque. The opening was narrow, but quite tall. It was almost as though an ancient giant had gashed the hillside with an ancient giant's knife. A small stream flowed outward from the opening and made a peaceful babble as it flowed over the rocky terrain. As far as Jerry was concerned, this might as well have been the doorway to another world.

A light breeze picked up, and he shivered. It was late April and the weather had been consistently warm, even hot on a few days. But out in these woods, under the shade of thick trees, an occasional chill would come through the air. It was the last words of a dying winter, whispered softly onto his skin. He rubbed at the gooseflesh on his bare arms and for the first time on the adventure, felt hesitation.

"Why'd you bring a rope?" Jerry looked over at John, who was winding a rope in a tight circle. He had also brought a homemade torch, a piece of flint, and a chunk of steel. Those things made sense, but the rope was something of a mystery.

"You'll see." John tightened the last loop of rope and secured it over his shoulder. "We're not getting any younger. Carry the torch for me. Now let's go find some treasure." With John leading the way, the two boys walked into the mouth of the old Missouri cave.

Once inside, the cave opened up considerably. The size was certainly exaggerated in their youthful eyes, but it was still an impressive space. The stream flowing out of the cave widened on the inside. It trickled along the far west wall, while the east side was a large open space, covered in rocky shell.

"Holy shit. This cave is as big as your butthole!" Jerry spun himself in a circle taking in its entirety.

"You're disgusting. Quit being an idiot and let's light the torch."

"Don't really need it, I can see really good in here." It was difficult to see how the light was getting in, but the cave was well-lit. You might have some trouble reading, or threading a needle, but it was quite sufficient to find your way around.

"It's not very bright in there." John motioned ahead. The stream ran out from a much smaller opening about twenty yards deeper into the cave. And man, did it ever look dark. So dark, in fact, Jerry hadn't even noticed it was there. He now felt a little more than hesitation; he felt fear. Apprehensively, he handed over the torch to his brother.

"You made that thing?"

"Sure did," John replied.

"It smells funny."

"That's the fuel I soaked the fabric in. Don't tell Mom I used some of her linen."

"Okay." Jerry's eyes were locked onto the small dark hallway ahead. "You're sure that thing's going to work? I mean, it smells like your butthole. Does your butthole catch fire?"

"Shut up." John carefully sat the torch on the ground and retrieved the flint and steel pieces from his breast pocket. He knelt beside the torch, and struck the pieces together, launching a spark. It was close, but landed a few inches to the right and fizzled out on a rock. He struck the steel again. Closer, but still a miss. On the third strike a large spark hit the wrapped end of the torch, and it ignited into a fireball.

"Whoa!" Jerry exclaimed, as John flashed a proud smile. For all his teasing, Jerry was pretty amazed by his big brother. And however scary that narrow opening might be, Jerry was going to follow him come hell or high water. As it turned out, it would be the latter.

The boys walked ahead to the opening. John was in the lead, holding out the torch. They felt like two medieval explorers traversing into the depths of a dark dungeon.

When they were close enough, John held the torch up high and illuminated a large portion of the path ahead. "The stream is over on the right side. If we stay to the left, we'll be on these rocks. It's like a path we can follow. Just hug the wall and stay in the light."

Jerry didn't respond. He followed the direction and stayed in lockstep behind his brother.

Once they entered the dark hallway, and it was illuminated by the torchlight, it wasn't quite as intimidating. There was more space than Jerry had envisioned, and his claustrophobic worries diminished. But they quickly came roaring back as the boys traversed further in.

The walls surrounding them started to narrow. The stream to their right grew wider and the rocky shell under their feet grew smaller. Before long they were almost walking sideways to stay on the rock, and their boots were splashing in the encroaching stream.

"What do we do now?" Jerry stammered. He hoped John would decide to turn around and go back, but there was no such luck.

"We get wet. Don't worry. It won't be for long."

"Really?"

"Really."

Jerry had an urge to turn and rush back on his own, but John had the torch. And bats. There could definitely be bats.

Jerry wanted to be brave, but he humbled himself. "I'm pretty scared."

Some big brothers could use that opportunity to poke fun at their sibling, but not John.

"Don't worry, I know what I'm doing." He put his free hand on Jerry's shoulder and looked at him reassuringly.

"What if the torch gets wet?"

"I could dip it in the stream and it would stay lit. That stuff that smells like my butthole is sulfur and lime. It keeps the torch lit even if it gets wet. Just like they used to use in castles."

Jerry didn't fully believe this claim, but it was enough to release the shackles of fear on his ankles. "Alright, let's do it." He grabbed a wad of John's shirt and followed behind as they waded into the water.

They walked against the current of the stream for what felt like an eternity. The cave seemed to grow tighter with every step. The water seemed to get colder. And most frightening of all, it seemed to

41

get deeper. 'Eternity' was actually fifteen minutes, but by the end of it the boys found themselves neck deep in cold cave water and facing a dead end. Jerry felt as though he would freeze to death before he made it out.

"I can't make it back, John. I'm too cold."

John was somehow looking enthusiastic. He had the same wild look that he had while inspecting those stupid pennies. "We're not going back. We're almost out. Hold the torch."

He handed the torch over.

"Hold it way up."

Jerry raised his arm as far as he could.

"Grab it with your other hand. Don't let go," John said, noticing his brother's wavering grip. He unfurled the rope and wrapped one end around Jerry's hand and closed it into a fist. "I'm going to go under and swim under this wall. In a few seconds I'll yank on the rope. When you feel me do that, you come too. Just don't let go."

Jerry did not like this plan whatsoever. But he could see there was not much choice in the matter. "What if you never pull the rope and you don't come back?"

"That won't happen. But if it does, just turn around and go back. It's not as cold as you think and it's not as far as you think. You'll be fine."

"And when I go under, what about the torch?"

"Just bring it with you underwater. It will go out, but you won't need it when you come up."

Jerry's brain was rapidly thinking of more questions, but he wasn't given the chance to voice them. John disappeared into the dark water, leaving Jerry alone. A horrifying wave of isolation came over him. He clutched the rope with a death grip. That rope was his only lifeline to a world outside of this cave. And as John had promised, after only a matter of seconds, there was a distinct tugging from somewhere on the other end.

Jerry took a deep breath and plunged himself into the water, extinguishing the torch and pulling himself along the rope. He emerged in a shower of light. Sounds of nature, sounds of outside, fell over him like a comforting blanket. He opened his eyes and found himself treading water in a small creek. The sun was shining down through the trees, the breeze felt warm, and his big brother John was taking him by the arm.

The boys laid down on the stony bank and stared up into the canopy. "How did you know you could swim under that wall?" Jerry asked, his breathing still labored from the swimming.

"Well, Nelson told me."

"He told you? *Told* you?"

"Yeah, he told me."

"He didn't show you?"

"No. It was the middle of winter. We would have frozen to death." John did not seem to think there was anything unusual about this. But to Jerry it was astounding. John had put complete faith and trust in the story of his friend. He had risked his life by simply going on Nelson's word. With that realization, Jerry felt as though his big brother must be one of the bravest men in the entire world.

Something glimmered in the corner of Jerry's eye, and he glanced over to the torch lying at his side. "You've got to be kidding me." It wasn't blazing, but the torch was still alight. A small thin sheet of blue flame roiled on the surface of the linen. With the last flames of the torch's life, John used it to make a campfire. They sat by it for the next hour, drying their clothes, warming their bones, and feeling nothing but love for each other.

5

One Wrong Step

The world is full of random occurrences. Or at least, seemingly random. Sometimes they are wonderful accidents. Other times they are cruel misfortunes. John often thought about the randomness of that day. The boys were always going to walk the same general path home, but their steps could have varied in a thousand different ways. They chose a path, with one wrong step, that would change their lives forever. Was it destiny? Or a random act of violence by mother nature?

"We didn't really look for the treasure," Jerry mused as the two boys walked home from the cave.

"Next time."

"You think there really is treasure?"

"Maybe. Don't see why not."

"I bet someone would have found it by now."

"You'd think, but people don't always look. That's how I found that penny."

Jerry smiled and considered his brother's wisdom. A breeze picked up, causing them both to shiver. The campfire had mostly dried out their clothes, but they were still damp. The sun was getting lower and less of its warm rays were breaking through the treetops.

At that moment, there was a large crunch from under Jerry's foot. The sound was loud enough to startle them both. They froze in their tracks and looked at each other. John would always remember feeling that time had slowed while they registered what happened. The crunch was followed by a buzzing sound. They felt a vibration in the air and under their feet.

"Run, Jerry." John looked at his brother with grave concern and felt the first bee sting break his skin. Jerry, also feeling the first few stings on his own skin, registered the danger they faced. He looked down and saw a large brown mass under the heel of his boot. It was moving and pulsing. It was alive and angry.

Jerry exploded into a mad sprint, and John followed quickly behind. There was a dark cloud chasing the boys and swirling around them. It thrummed with hostility. The pair were running faster than they ever had, but it was no match for the speed of the bees. One sting became three. Three became six. Six became a dozen.

The dark, thrumming cloud of small yellow assassins had mostly coalesced around Jerry. They made him feel more enclosed than the walls of the cave. He had been so scared inside the narrow hall of that cave, but he'd give anything to be back there now. He'd give anything to trade these bees in for bats.

Jerry felt desperate for air and sucked in a hot breath. In horror, he realized more bees entered his mouth than air. He could feel their bodies thrashing around his throat. Hot needles of pain pierced his tongue. Every part of his body felt like it was swelling. And despite his racing heart, he felt like his blood had been replaced with a thickening and sickly sludge. Within the dark, buzzing cloud, he thought he heard John call out to him. But he would never find out; the sound of the furious bees drowned out all else until his world turned black.

***

"Get up, Jerry!" John raced to his brother's side and tried to shelter Jerry's body with his own. He looked down at his face and saw it was almost unrecognizable. His head looked like a melon that had been sitting out in the hot sun and was on the verge of popping.

"Jesus, Jerry!" John gasped and felt a rampaging bee slide into his mouth. He bit down and felt its pulsing body crush between his teeth. A warm, bitter ooze gushed out onto his tongue.

John picked his brother up, threw him over his shoulder, and then he ran. He ran with everything his body could manage. Despite Jerry's weight and the persistence of the attacking bees, John moved with considerable speed. He ran and ran and ran.

When he could finally see their home and heard the sound of his father chopping wood he began to scream. And then there was blackness.

John awoke in a strange room. He could feel the sensation of a cool rag on his forehead. His father was sitting at the foot of the bed and had a hand gently resting on his leg. John's first thought was how much older the man looked. His skin appeared tight, almost leathery. His eyes were damp and sunken. John had never seen his father cry, but it was apparent he had been doing so recently.

"Where am I?" John said in a raspy voice. His throat felt like it was filled with shattered glass. He coughed and put his hand to his neck.

"Here, take a sip of water." His father was visibly excited to see him awake. He held a tin cup to his mouth and tipped it just enough that John could feel the cool water touch his dry lips. He reached for the cup and tried to tip more water into his mouth.

"Slow down, not too much," his father said. "You're at Doctor Morton's in town. You've been here for a week. In and out. Mostly out."

"A week?" John fought hard to piece together the last things he remembered.

"Yes, a week. A little more, actually. We thought we'd lost you...." His father's words trailed off.

"What? What were you about to say?" John's heart sank into his stomach as his mind was clearing.

"What do you remember, son?"

"I showed Jerry a cave that Nelson told me about. We were heading home and he made a wrong step. He crushed a beehive. I don't know if they built it on the ground or if it fell..." John trailed

47

off this time and grabbed his throat. His father grabbed the tin cup and helped him get another drink of water. "You were going to say lost us both." John locked on to his father's eyes.

"Yes son, I was. We lost him." Tears were bursting from the man's eyes and trickling down his stubbled cheeks.

"Jerry can't be dead. It was just bees. Just stupid bees!" This was all too shocking to comprehend and John hoped he might still be feverish and dreaming.

"Dr. Morton said you both seem to have an aversion to the bee venom. Anyone would as many times as they stung you, but you two more than normal, I guess. And especially Jerry."

John reached out and grabbed his father's hand, tears trickling down his face. "This is my fault. I should have saved him. I should have found some way to save him."

"This is not your fault, son!" John's father wiped at his eyes. His voice was shaking, but full of sincerity. "It's just like you said. It was just one wrong step. God will lead us through this."

"You and mother don't blame me?"

"No, of course not. We don't blame you. We love you. You gave everything you had to save Jerry. You must have carried him over a mile on your shoulder getting stung hundreds, hell maybe thousands of times. I don't think I would have made it as far as you did. Your mom is at home right now, probably praying that you will be okay. And now her prayers are answered."

"Well, look who's with us." A spectacled man entered the room, beaming at the sight of John awake and talking. "Did you give him water?" Dr. Morton asked John's father, who nodded in confirmation. "Good, not too much. It's going to take a while for his body to start working like normal again."

Dr. Morton stood over John and removed the damp rag from his forehead. He pressed the skin around his neck before feeling his forehead with the back of his hand. "You're still a bit swollen and feeling like you fell off a cliff I imagine."

"Yes. Everything hurts."

"That's normal. Going to be that way for a while, I'm afraid. But now that you've come through, I think you're going to be okay." Dr. Morton smiled and his glasses slipped down his nose. "Get some rest, young man, while your father goes to fetch your mother. She's going to want to know you're doing better."

John closed his eyes and pictured Jerry's face. He could see the two of them back at the creek, sitting by the campfire in their underwear. Their clothes and boots were drying by the fire, and they were still beaming from their adventure in the cave. John realized that would always be one of the best moments in his entire life. A life that wouldn't be the same without his little brother Jerry.

Sleep came and John dreamed. He was standing with Jerry on a ground made of rocky shell, much like was in the cave. But they were not in the cave. They were not in the woods. There was nothing but openness around them. It was nighttime and the sky overhead was a rich black. They were in their underwear and holding hands, gazing up at the stars. Were they stars? No, they were *lights*. The sky was filled with them. They were all the colors John had ever seen and colors he didn't even know existed. They danced and swirled and glowed. They were radiant flaming orbs, stretched out as far as his eyes could see.

"They are so beautiful, Jerry." John looked down at his little brother. When Jerry looked up to reply, John could see that his face was grotesquely swollen. His cheeks and forehead had expanded so much the skin was starting to split and eke out a foul-smelling yellow mucous. Where his eyes should have been there were two barely visible slits of skin.

"He comes with the lights. And he is death, John." Jerry's mouth opened wider and for a moment John thought his brother was about to scream. But instead, bees poured out between his lips and into the night. They made an awful buzzing sound and John felt the familiar vibration their wings made on the air. A blinding white light began to shine out through the slits of Jerry's eyes. It filled John's entire vision, and then he awoke again.

He was still in the same bed at Dr. Morton's, but this time his father wasn't in the room. He could see from the window it was night outside. Plump beads of rain were trickling down the windowpane. John was scared and restless, but would eventually drift back to sleep. His body would recover quickly from that point on, and he'd never remember that particular dream again.

Part Two
The Roads That Change Us

"I thought I was whole

When you were with me

The sick in my head

Has taken you from me.

Now, no more dreams.

This nightmare is here to stay.

Here to stay.

Here to stay." – A Mixtape Catastrophe, Reprise

1

You Taste Like Salt

Wesley Nelson did not like to camp. It felt beneath him. A man of his skill should always have a roof over his head. And most often, he did have a roof over his head. But not this morning.

Wesley maneuvered out from his lean-to and stood up. He stretched out his muscles and made an almost comical yawn. The temperature was perfect for May. The summer heat had not yet set

51

in. Mornings like this one, in the Iowa woods, still had a slight chill in the air.

Scratching at his crotch through the fabric of his long johns, Wesley walked over to the coals of a small fire. He was cold during the night and uncomfortable, but it was important to keep the fire small. That was another drawback of having to set up camp. It was never his land, and there was always the risk of discovery. Discovery always led to unwanted attention and conflict. Wesley enjoyed conflict, but only when he could dictate the terms.

He stoked at the ashy grey coals until some small flames started to re-emerge. He added some of the kindling he set out the night before and rebuilt the campfire, just enough to warm his hands and boil a small pot of tea.

Beneath him or not, it was hard not to appreciate some aspects of being out in the woods. Wesley drank his hot tea, breathed in tendrils of campfire smoke, and took in the majesty of the woods. At night, the surrounding forest had a surreal quality. He often thought there were witches in the woods, probably watching him. He thought of himself as a witch, too. A warlock. A high priest of black magic. He would sometimes make this admission to women before they died at his hands. And what was his magic? It was killing. That was the greatest magic of all.

Wesley's most recent conquest in Missouri had gotten a little messy, even for him. He came remarkably close to being apprehended. So he started venturing further North and exploring new stomping grounds. He had barely crossed the border into Altoon, Iowa when he came upon a small farmhouse on the outskirts of town.

He had cautiously worked his way close to the home. His initial mindset was on stealing a horse so he could make better time moving North. But a blonde-haired woman named Elanor Slater would change his plans.

He saw her behind the farmhouse. She was rinsing clothing in a large, galvanized tub. She wore a homely white dress, which wouldn't be flattering to any woman's figure. But Wesley could see the potential beneath. In his mind's eye, he could see the pale skin of her breasts. They were heaving and sweating as a frightened heart pounded beneath her skin. She was restrained by the very clothesline she was about to hang her laundry on. She was completely helpless and ready to be taken apart.

Thud! A door slammed, and Wesley realized his hand was stroking his penis through his pants. He looked around nervously to ensure he was still unseen. The slamming door had been a large balding man coming out of the farmhouse. He was overweight, but quite muscular. Wesley assumed this was the woman's husband. He'd need to be dealt with quickly when the time came. And the time would come. The fever was on him now.

He needed to get going, but he stole a few more glances at Elanor before moving on. The husband had approached her, briefly discussed something, then walked back into the house. Elanor stood up and rested her hands on her hips. Locks of her yellow hair blew in the wind. *I'll need to cut some of that hair off*, Wesley thought. *The whole scalp maybe*. Oh yes, the fever was on.

He avoided Altoon and made a small makeshift camp about two miles south of the Slater's farmland. Several times a day, for the next three days, he'd work his way back and forth through the wooded areas of the farm that provided cover and keep a close eye on the Slaters. For the most part, they seemed to have a consistent routine. Wesley's sample size was small, but he thought he'd seen enough to know his opening.

The campfire made a hissing sound as he extinguished it with the last water in his teapot. He ran his fingers through his oily red hair and let the white campfire smoke envelop his body. Today would be the day. It would have to be. Because when the fever was on, only killing, raping, and taking apart could calm the storm in his soul.

Elanor's husband, David, had a large wooden rocking chair you might expect to find on a porch. Yet he preferred to keep it in the grass, about ten yards from the house, in what you might consider the Slater's front yard. Every morning, shortly after sunrise, he would spend about twenty minutes in his rocking chair, enjoying a cup of coffee. May 11th, 1897 was no different. He faced a long day of tending to his maturing wheat fields and dairy cows.

Cows were a new venture for David's farm and he had only purchased them last month. The cows gave him increased financial anxiety, but mostly he was confident the investment would be worthwhile. Those ten cows were the last thing David thought about before realizing his throat had been slit open from behind. He was bleeding to death in his favorite rocking chair.

David's head plopped forward, and he could see blood flowing down his overalls and pooling in his portly lap. For a frightening moment, he thought Elanor must have been his killer. Why would she do this? Why would she sneak up behind him and cut him open? Was she angry with him and he didn't know it? But those concerns were dismissed when a hand covered his mouth and a male voice whispered in his ear.

"Death awaits you, fat fuck." Wesley spoke softly, almost affectionately. And despite being a whisper, the heavy southern accent was still evident in his voice. "There will only be death. No god. No devil. I'm the alpha and omega and I've chosen your wife to serve me."

David tried to scream and warn Elanor, but only gurgling noises came out from his mouth. With a final bubbling sound from his throat, he closed his eyes and died.

Before slicing open David's throat, Wesley had been crouched down on the side of the porch, waiting for him to come out and start his morning routine. Wesley now retook this position and made a series of loud banging knocks on the wooden planks of the porch. Elanor came out of the house asking David what the ruckus was. When he didn't respond, she approached him in the rocking chair. David's back was to the house, and Wesley thought from this vantage point you couldn't really tell that something was wrong. He clamped a hand to his mouth to dampen a psychotic giggle.

When Elanor was just a few feet away from the rocking chair, he emerged from his cover. This time, his bloody hunting knife was sheathed, and he was wielding a small wooden club instead. He struck Elanor on the back of the head and she tumbled to the ground, unconscious. The yellowing sleeping gown she was wearing had come undone, and Wesley could see she wasn't wearing any underwear. It was all he could do to not have her right there in the yard. He took a breath, steadied his shaking hands, and put the club in his back pocket.

First, he picked up Elanor's unconscious body. She was a petite woman, and he was able to get her inside the house with ease. He placed her on the floor of their kitchen area, and then went back outside and dumped David out of the rocking chair. It was unlikely anyone would happen upon the farm and discover the murder, but he still felt it was smart to move him. Much the opposite of Elanor, it took all he had to move David's corpse. He barely managed to drag him to the side of the farmhouse. He then tipped over a rick of firewood, mostly concealing the body.

When Wesley came back into the house, Elanor was moaning and starting to writhe around on the floor. She was trying to reach for her head, but kept missing the target and flailing her arms around. This struck Wesley as comical, and he let out a giggle, this time not bothering to cover his mouth.

"Oh, you dumb bitch. You look drunk, you know that?" He straddled her and further separated the front opening of her gown.

55

David had some tools sitting on the kitchen floor, and two particular items caught Wesley's attention. There was a large woodworking hammer and some carpentry nails. He had a fetish for ropes and bindings, but now he had the idea of nailing Elanor to the kitchen floor. He wasn't sure if it would work, but it sounded exciting.

"What's your name?" He slapped Elanor in the face several times and pulled up on her eyelids.

"What? What? What?" she asked in a pitiful and whining voice.

"I said tell me your fucking name!"

"Elanor! It's Elanor!"

"Oh, that's pretty." Pretty sounded more like *purdy*. "I usually like to tie a woman up. Tie 'em to the bed. But I think I'm going to crucify you, Elanor. Except instead of a cross, it's going to be right here on this kitchen floor. And I'm going to spread your legs out real wide before I nail your feet down. That's so I can fuck you. You think that will work?" Wesley flashed a smile of jagged, yellowing teeth.

"I don't understand. Why are you doing this?"

"Why? Why? What a stupid fucking question!" Wesley looked at her with disappointment. And then, in an instant, his expression changed to a prideful glow. "Because I'm a Warlock, Elanor. And you are my sacrifice." Still straddling her, he reached over and grabbed the hammer and a handful of the large nails. He placed the nails in his mouth and clamped down with his teeth. He took a moment to savor the rusty taste of the iron. A carpenter by trade, these tools felt familiar and good. He raised her hands above her head, then shuffled up so his knees were pinning her arms.

Elanor jerked her head side to side, thrashing her body. "No, no, no, please no!"

"Quit moving you fucking bitch or I'll put this nail through one of your eyeballs."

His threat worked, and the young woman stopped moving. An occasional whimper escaped her mouth, but she remained still. Wesley placed the tip of the nail against her open palm. He grinned; an expression that was short-lived when he heard a voice calling outside.

"Fuck," Wesley hissed. He grabbed his club and struck Elanor again. Her body went limp beneath him. Satisfied she was unconscious, he scanned the room, desperately searching for a hiding place. There was a large wooden hutch in the back corner of their living area. It was positioned far enough from the wall that a slender man, like Wesley, could squeeze behind it. He did so quickly, then quietly unsheathed his hunting knife. He waited patiently as a male voice continued to call from the outside.

"Elanor? David? Hello?" A large man peered in through the front window. "Your front door is not closed all the way. Are you here?" He continued to call out as he strained to see through dirty panes of glass. Wesley thought there was a slow sound to the man's voice. He had to be retarded. "Elanor, is that your foot? Are you hurt, Miss Elanor?" The man's voice elevated in panic, and he pushed open the front door.

He could see Elanor sprawled out on the kitchen floor and unconscious. He rushed over and knelt beside her. "Miss Elanor, what's wrong? Where's David?" He wiped sweaty strands of hair from Elanor's face, before his eyes drifted to the hammer beside her. "Was there some kind of accident?"

Wesley peered in disbelief from behind the hutch. David, Elanor's husband, was a large man. He was fat, yes, but clearly strong from a lifetime of hard work. This retarded man, by comparison, was absolutely massive. His enormous frame set on top of legs like oak trees. His plain white shirt was too small for his torso and Wesley imagined it must be hard for such a large man to find proper fitting clothes.

He was big enough to give Wesley a great deal of hesitation about attacking him. His hunting knife was drawn and Wesley felt confident he'd have the element of surprise, but if he made a misstep, it could prove problematic. He was in the midst of this contemplation when his eyes widened at the unfolding scene. The retarded man had leaned over and started to kiss Elanor on the lips.

"You naughty little pervert," Wesley whispered and again found himself trying to stifle laughter.

"I thought maybe if I kissed you Miss Elanor it might wake you up." The man ran his finger across Elanor's lips. He looked around the room to ensure they were alone. He then knelt over again and started to lick the sweat off Elanor's face. "You sure do taste like salt, Miss Elanor. I like salt. I like you. I've always liked you." He stood up and undid the button on his pants. He took another look around the room, then dropped his pants, revealing a huge erect penis.

Wesley had thought this was all hilarious at first. But now this fucking retarded cocksucker was going to spoil his prize. "I'm going to lop that thing off you, big boy." Wesley soundlessly mouthed and squeezed the hilt of his knife.

The man spread Elanor's legs apart and positioned himself between them. "I don't know what happened, Miss Elanor, but I'm hoping this might help you wake up. I bet David hurt you didn't he?" He rubbed at his penis and stared into Elanor's swollen eyes. He was just about to insert his penis into her, and Wesley was just about to slit his throat, when something happened that surprised them both.

Elanor's eyes opened wide and she began to scream. She started striking him on the side of the head. "Leave me alone! Leave me alone, Spencer!" The huge man, who could easily choke the life out of her, recoiled in fear. He threw up his hands defensively and tried to stand up.

59

"Stop, Elanor! Stop! I'm trying to help you!" Spencer yelled while trying to pull up his pants.

"Help me with your dick out, Spencer? Where is David? What is happening to me?" Elanor was screaming, crying, punching, and kicking. Wesley started to emerge again, but saw that Spencer had spun around and would be facing him directly. The man's enormous size again caused Wesley to hesitate.

Spencer continued working to pull up his pants and at the same time made his way to the front door. He stumbled several times, but eventually managed to secure his pants and scramble outside. Elanor continued to pursue him, screaming and striking at him. Spencer ran away from the Slater Farm, into the street, and towards the town of Altoon. Elanor, crazed and disoriented, pursued him.

Wesley was agitated and frantic. He looked around the Slater home for anything he wanted to take. "Stupid fucking retard! Fuck!" His anger at this turn of events was building and his vision started to blur he was so enraged. He took a moment to steady himself. "Breathe, just breathe." He opened a drawer in their bedroom and found some of Elanor's undergarments. He wadded them up and stuffed them into his pants. He then fled the farm and made his way back to his makeshift camp.

As he sat next to the previous night's dead campfire, he buried his face in Elanor's panties. He had been preparing himself to pack up and leave, but Wesley knew that couldn't be allowed. When he wanted something, he'd get it. When a Warlock sets his eyes on a woman, he should have her. And wouldn't the retard be blamed for everything that has happened? Was Elanor even coherent enough to realize she had two attackers? Wesley thought there was a good chance her brain was scrambled enough to blame it all on the retard. He'd stay in camp for a few more days, watch from afar, and then take one more shot at getting his prize.

2

The Vaquero

"That's the first time I've made it with a black man." Sheila looked over at the rugged, dark-skinned cowboy.

"And? How was it?" The cowboy worked to light a large cigar.

"Best I've ever had. Wish all my customers could be black men." Sheila caressed the man's bare chest.

The cowboy took a large puff from his cigar and leaned back on the bed frame. "It's not a black thing, baby."

"What do you mean?"

"It's a me thing. I'm the best you ever had."

"You're saying all black men aren't as good as you?"

"Hell no. Black, white, and anything in-between. I'm just the best there is."

"You were so gentle. I think that's what made you different."

"How else should a beautiful woman be treated, if not gentle?" The cowboy turned to look at her. In those eyes, he could see a hundred men before him who had not been so caring.

"I didn't get your name."

"Don't really have one. Most just call me Vaquero."

"Vaquero?"

"Yes."

"What's that mean?"

"A Vaquero is a Mexican cowboy." The Vaquero waited for the standard response he had become accustomed to.

"But you aren't—"

"Mexican?" he interrupted.

"Right."

"I spent some time there. In Mexico. Made some good friends. That's what they called me."

"You don't know your real name?"

The Vaquero thought back through his own less gentle memories. "I know it. Just got no use for it." He took another large drag from his cigar.

A series of knocks came from the door. "Vaquero, you in there?"

The Vaquero reached over to the bedstand and grabbed the handle of his revolver. "Who's asking?" he shouted, handing the cigar to the prostitute.

"Sheriff Downy."

"There some kind of trouble?"

"Not with you. But there is trouble. I'm hoping to get your help. I'm sorry if I'm...interrupting. But it's important. A man is dead, a woman is hurt, and there's a killer on the loose."

The Vaquero sighed. He massaged the bridge of his nose with his thumb and forefinger. "Let me get dressed. I'll meet you in the lobby in ten minutes."

"Great. See you then." The Sheriff sounded nervous, but relieved.

Ten minutes later, The Vaquero and Sheriff Downy sat across from each other at a small table in the hotel lobby. Sheriff Downy was tall, thin, and balding. Despite his age, he gave off an air of inexperience. He was fidgety and rubbing his hands together in a nervous tick.

The Vaquero was much the opposite. He was a man you'd instinctively give a wide berth to on the street. He sat completely still and stared down the Sheriff. His large cowboy hat seemed to cast a shadow across the room. The Vaquero could feel eyes on him. Some may have been inquisitive, but others may have recognized him as the infamous bounty hunter of the frontier. The man who'd seen everything. The man who'd done everything.

The Vaquero rubbed at the stubble on his face. "I intended to get a shave this morning. Do you think we can get on with whatever this is?"

Sheriff Downy cleared his throat. "Yes."

He took a moment to scan the room. He looked to the front door and acknowledged his deputy, who was standing patient and attentive.

"A passing wagon found one of our residents, Elanor Slater, passed out on the road. She had been beaten. She was half-naked. Raped maybe, we aren't sure. They brought her to me. When she woke up, she was disoriented, crazed. It was all the doctor could do to calm her down." The Sheriff paused for a moment, then pulled a flask from his jacket pocket. He popped off the cap and knocked back a swig.

"It's a little early don't you think?" The Vaquero laughed.

"It's necessary today I'm afraid," the man muttered, holding the flask out.

The Vaquero stared for a moment, then took the flask and knocked back a swig. "Continue," he said handing it back to the Sheriff.

"We finally got her to talk. She was confused about what happened, but thought she'd been attacked by two men. She remembered going outside to check on her husband David, but then she woke up on the floor in her house. There was a man with red hair on top of her. She said he was real ugly, but kind of baby-faced. She said he was going to rape her. She said—" the Sheriff took another swig. "She said he was going to nail her hands and feet to the floor."

"Jesus," the Vaquero muttered. "No pun intended. You said a pair? Where's the other man?"

"That's where the story gets stranger. We've got a local man, Spencer Braden. He's not quite right."

"What does that mean?"

"In the head. He wasn't born right. He's retarded. That word always feels mean to me, but that's what he is."

"I see. And how does this retarded man play into things?"

"Spencer is a farmer without a farm. He lives way out North in a small place his parents left to him. He comes into town and picks up work at the local farms. He's retarded, but he does well enough finding hard work and taking care of himself."

"Was he at the farm with Elanor?"

"He showed up, yes. According to her, Spencer began calling out while the man with red hair was attacking her. She thought that Spencer might save her, or at least find David. But when she awoke, it was Spencer trying to rape her. She started beating on him and chased him from the house. That's the last thing she remembers. Running down the road screaming at Spencer. She must have passed out again, until the wagon passed by and she got brought to me."

"Up at my room, you said a man was killed. Who was it, the husband?"

"Yes." The Sheriff took another swig and offered it to The Vaquero, who refused.

"We might have a long day ahead of us, Sheriff. Slow down on that."

"You're right." The Sheriff slipped the flask back into his jacket pocket, hanging his head ashamedly.

"The husband..."

"Yes, David. My deputy rode out to the Slater Farm. The house showed signs of a struggle. He found a hammer and nails on the kitchen floor where Elanor said she'd been attacked. He also found David. His throat was slit and somebody had covered up his body with firewood on the side of the house."

The Vaquero looked over to the deputy and motioned him over to the table. "The Sheriff tells me you found the husband, David."

"Yes, sir." The deputy nodded. He was young, clean-cut, and seemingly more in control of himself than the Sheriff.

"His throat was cut?"

"Yes, it was a pretty terrible thing to see."

"I can imagine."

"He's got a rocking chair set up in the yard, in front of his house. It was covered in blood. And I found a trail of blood going from the chair to the side of the house where I found the body. I think someone killed him in his chair. From behind, I reckon. Then dragged him over."

"And whoever did this, tried to hide the body?"

"Yes, covered him up with firewood. They have a rack on the side of the house. It was just dumped over on top of him."

The Vaquero pondered for a moment. "Anything else you want me to know?"

"Yes. David Slater, he was a big man. Would take somebody pretty strong to move him like that."

"This Spencer Braden, he strong enough?"

Both Sheriff Downy and the deputy's eyes widened, and they looked at each other. "Yes," they said in unison, nodding their heads.

"So, he's big I take it? Big and strong?"

"Very," said Sheriff Downy.

The Vaquero took off his cowboy hat and sat it down on the table. He rubbed his temples for a moment, while he considered the evidence. The Vaquero, who was normally shaved bald, also had some light stubble popping up on his scalp.

"Most retarded folk I know are friendly. Like children. Is this like him to do such a terrible thing?"

"He's not violent." said the Sheriff. "Never has been. But from time to time, I've received complaints."

"What kind of complaints?"

"Some people in town have caught him peeping. Spying on women. He just makes some folks uncomfortable. Most of the time he gets a pass because of his, uhm, condition. But I've had to keep some husbands from going after him a time or two. About a year ago I caught him looking in one of the windows at this hotel. He was—" The Sheriff lowered his voice. "...He was playing with himself. I kept it quiet, but I got on him pretty good. Haven't had any trouble since." The Sheriff again looked ashamed.

"Don't feel guilty, Sheriff. You was just trying to do the man a kindness." The Vaquero's voice was sincere. He was known for many things; his bravery, his toughness, but also his compassion

and his honor. The latter was on display here. "Where is Spencer now? Did you pick him up?"

"No. He fled. I heard you were here and that's why I sought you out. I figured if someone would know how to catch him. It'd be you."

"And the man with red hair. We know anything about him?"

"No. Nothing. Don't even know if he's real."

"I know of one killer with red hair. Baby faced. He's not one I've been hunting for. And he's usually further south. But it's possible. Could I speak with Elanor?"

"She's pretty distraught. But yes, of course. I'm sure she'd do anything to find Spencer and this other man."

Not thirty minutes later, The Vaquero would find himself sitting in the small Sheriff's office face to face with Elanor Slater. It was always hard for him to see folks in pain. In many ways, he felt as though he could feel their anguish. He could feel everything they'd been through. All they'd suffered. It quieted his own pain, which was a blessing, but he couldn't stand to see others in so much despair. It fueled his need to hunt. To take bad men out of the world. To see them locked away or strung up.

Elanor looked exhausted. She sat on a small cot, wrapped in a blanket. Her blonde hair was pulled back in a ponytail. She had wide eyes, like those of a deer. They were curious, but untrusting eyes. And who could blame her after all she'd been through?

"Who are you?" Elanor asked.

"Folks call me The Vaquero. I'm a bounty hunter." He anticipated the usual question and answer routine about his namesake, but it did not come.

"You going to catch the men who did this to me?"

"I'm going to try. It's what I'm good at. You sure it's *men*?" The Vaquero was afraid this question might insult her, so he made sure his tone was kind and genuine.

"Yes, it was two men. The first one I don't know. He was hideous, but kind of baby-faced. Red hair, freckles, jagged teeth. He was cruel." A small tear ran down Elanor's face. "The other man was Spencer Braden, the retard that helps on the farm. I don't think the two of them were together. I think Spencer being there was just, just an accident." She wiped the tear from her face.

"Who do you think hurt David?"

"The man with red hair. I think Spencer's only interest was me. And when he found me like that, helpless, he just saw a chance to have his way with me. I don't think it's in Spencer to kill. But I don't know."

"Where did the man with red hair go, you think? Why didn't he go after Spencer if they weren't together?"

"You must not have ever seen Spencer. He's as big as an ox. Scared the other man off I would imagine."

"Yeah, I've heard he's a big old boy."

"One last thing, Elanor. I'm sorry to bring this up. But the man with red hair, you say he was going to nail your hands and feet to the floor?"

"Yes." Elanor closed her eyes for a moment and paused. It clearly took courage to remember. Looking back on that sort of memory felt like handling a stick of dynamite in your hands, waiting for it to go off. "He said he usually likes to tie a woman up, but that he was going to crucify me instead."

The Vaquero's eyes widened. "Did he say anything else about that? Tying you up?"

"That was it, that he liked to tie women up to the bed. Does that mean something to you?"

"Maybe. I've heard about a man that does that. Thank you, Elanor." The Vaquero stood up and started to walk towards the door. He paused, then turned back. "I've seen a lot of bad things in my time, Elanor. Experienced a lot of bad things. But strong people like you. Like me. We get through it. If you put your mind to it, you'll get through this darkness and come out on the other side." Elanor thought this over for a moment, then gave a single nod of agreement.

"Sheriff, grab your bounty tickets and meet me outside." Sitting on the steps of the Sheriff's office, The Vaquero sifted through a stack of wanted posters. The Sheriff and the deputy watched curiously. "Here, this one." The Vaquero handed one of the posters over to Sheriff Downy.

The Sheriff read aloud, "Wesley Nelson, also known as the Missouri Mauler. Also known as the Babyface Killer."

"That's right. Red-haired asshole. Done a lot of killing south of you. It don't say it on that poster, but there's something else I've heard about him."

"What's that?"

The Vaquero fell silent, trying to muster the correct words. "Me and some of the other hunters, we've talked about our tickets before. Things we see as patterns. A lot of these men do the same things over and over again. It's almost like their crimes have their signature on them." The Sheriff and the deputy nodded, seeming to grasp this concept. "Wesley Nelson, I'm told, has a thing for ropes. Ties most of his victims to the bed while he does the devil's work.

The men he usually kills quick and gets them out of the way. But sometimes he ties them up too."

"So what are you thinking here?"

"I'm thinking Elanor's got it right. I think Wesley made his way up to Iowa and had his eye on her. He made his move and all was going to plan until Spencer happened to show up and create a mess all his own. In the chaos, Wesley decided to slip away. Probably moving North, looking for his next opportunity. He hasn't been one of my tickets, but I think I'll be looking for him now."

"And Spencer?"

"I think you boys are going to find Spencer hasn't gone far at all."

"We checked his place. No sign of him of there."

"Don't check it again. Just stay away. Let me take care of Spencer. Sheriff, you stay here with Elanor and do your best to take care of her. Deputy, I never caught your name?"

"Johnny, sir."

"Johnny, can you pick up an extra hand, get Elanor's place cleaned up? Get David's body back here so it can be properly taken care of?"

"I can."

"Good. I'll be back by tomorrow if I'm right. I'll need to keep my horse here, with yours. That a problem?"

"Not at all. Behind the office here. You'll find a small stable."

"Good. Now tell me how to find Spencer's place."

The men all did as instructed. Deputy Johnny grabbed a friend from town and they worked all evening to clean up the mess at the Slater Farm. The next morning, they did the gruesome work of loading David onto a wagon and hauling his corpse back into town. The Sheriff stayed with Elanor. He kept her warm and fed, although she wouldn't eat much. She would drink, however, and he kept her supplied with coffee. At her request, each cup would get a dash of whiskey from his flask.

The Vaquero gathered his things from the hotel room and gave Sheila the prostitute a parting kiss. He then stabled his horse with the Sheriff's, before heading towards the property of Spencer Braden on foot. He'd reach the house within a couple of hours, and watch cautiously for two more hours, before discreetly slipping inside.

***

Spencer had spent the past sixteen hours in the woods near his home. After the incident with Miss Elanor, he'd went straight there, but was reluctant to go inside. Spencer was certain men would be looking for him and he didn't want to get trapped. He also didn't know where else to go. So he waited and he watched.

Night came, and he had almost built up enough courage to go home when he saw the Sheriff and his deputy ride up on horseback. They made their way into his house and spent at least an hour inside, before they went looking around the property by lamp light. Eventually they rode on back towards Altoon. Spencer again found himself shaken and decided to wait longer.

The night grew cold, but he didn't dare start a fire. He also feared there might be witches in the woods. They might be watching him. They might want to harm him. He would close his eyes and sing to himself. *The sun will rise, the sun will set.. How fast go by the days.* He resisted the urge to go inside and waited through the night.

By the next night, no one else had come. He knew this was his best chance to gather some things and leave. Did he have to leave? Maybe men wouldn't come again and he could stay at the home? Part of him thought this was reasonable, but another part knew it was foolish. He had done a bad thing. Maybe worse than things he'd done before. And this time, the Sheriff wasn't likely to let him go. He might get locked up in jail. Or even hung. Good Lord, could he be hung?

Spencer's belly grumbled from hunger. His mouth felt dry, like cotton, but it began to salivate as he got closer to his front door. He was thinking about the salted beef in his pantry and the bucket of well water by his bed. It consumed his thoughts and pushed away those of imprisonment or hanging. He made his way inside and went first for the water in his bedroom.

He grabbed an empty cup from his nightstand and was about to dip it in the bucket when he heard a match striking. Startled, he spun around and saw a man sitting in his living room. Through the glow of a burning cigar, Spencer could see it was a black man wearing a large, dark cowboy hat. The man wasn't wearing a badge, but he had the impression of a lawman.

"Don't stop on account of me. If you're thirsty, get a drink." The man puffed on the large cigar. Spencer frowned and looked down at the empty cup in his hands. "You've been hiding out in the woods a long time. I imagine you are quite thirsty."

"I am thirsty, mister."

"Then drink."

Spencer did so, scooping up one, then two cups of water and gulping them down, "You here for me, mister?"

"I am."

"Are you gonna kill me, mister?"

"I'm a bounty hunter. Most tickets have an option of dead or alive. And I usually choose dead. There's less risk that way. But truth is, there ain't a ticket on you yet. So I figure I'll just bring you in and let the law figure out what's next."

"You think I might hang?"

"Tough to say. Did you kill anybody?"

"No, sir!" Spencer stepped forward and was illuminated by some of the moonlight coming through a window.

"Who killed David then?"

"David is...David is dead?" Spencer's eyes widened. The bounty hunter stared, silently smoking his cigar. "I didn't know David was dead sir."

"Well, you did try to rape Elanor. You admit that much?"

"I just, I just wanted to make her feel better."

The man scowled. "You might be slow, Spencer, but I think you know better than that. Putting your dick in a woman who don't want it there ain't no way to make her feel better."

Spencer took a moment to contemplate. "I do. My daddy always called me something mean. He said I was a pervert and that I had to keep that part of me under control. But sometimes, I can't control it. Miss Elanor is just so pretty. I didn't want to hurt her. Can they hang me for what I did?" Spencer was speaking at a frantic pace.

"Yes. They can." The bounty hunter stood up. "Did you see anyone else at the Slater Farm?"

"No, sir. Not a soul."

"Alright. We're going to head into town and face whatever comes next. You going to give me any trouble?"

"No, sir," Spencer whimpered, tears filling his eyes.

"Stop that now. You do a lot of thinking about yourself. Retarded or not, that's a poor quality in a man."

"Yes, sir." Spencer wiped his nose and tried to hold back more tears.

"Get another drink of water, it's a long walk. You stay in front of me the whole time. You got a gun?"

"No, sir."

"Good. I do." The bounty hunter patted his sidearm in its holster. "And on this little walk, if you ever make me feel nervous, or do anything stupid, I'm going to put a bullet in the back of your skull. Then whatever they decide won't matter. They don't hang corpses. You understand?"

"Yes, sir." Spencer downed another cup of water and the two men set out for town.

***

The following night The Vaquero found himself standing at the back of a large crowd, next to the Sheriff. Spencer Braden, retarded and given to perversion, was standing on the town gallows. A black cloth was pulled over his head and his hands were bound behind his back.

"Justice moves fast here," The Vaquero remarked to the Sheriff.

"It does. In matters like this. Not that we have many matters like this." The two men watched fixedly on the proceedings.

"Spencer Braden has been accused and admitted to the attempted rape of Elanor Slater. We believe Elanor had been previously assaulted by the known killer Wesley Nelson and was in a state of helplessness. Instead of rescuing Elanor, Spencer took it upon himself to further violate her. Because of this, we have seen fit to sentence Spencer Braden to death. Mr. Braden, do you have any last words?" The executioner looked towards Spencer, who remained silent and shook his head. He could be heard sobbing through the thin fabric veil.

A few moments later, the executioner pulled a lever and released a trap door under Spencer's feet. There was a large snapping sound as his neck broke and a farting noise as he shit his pants. Spencer's gigantic form was more weight than his neck could withstand. Just seconds after his neck snapped, it completely separated from his body and his headless corpse fell to the ground. The crowd of onlookers gasped and turned away from the grotesque sight. Elanor, standing at the front of the crowd, did not look away. She instead slowly clapped, spit on the ground, then turned and walked back to the Sheriff's office.

The Vaquero watched all this with a heavy heart. Spencer had done a terrible thing. He had proven he was dangerous. But given the man's low intellect, The Vaquero questioned if this truly was justice.

There was a few long minutes of silence before the two men spoke. "We bury David in a few days. Elanor wants to go back to her house until then. What do you think?" the Sheriff inquired of The Vaquero.

"I don't think she should be alone. I think Wesley has gone. But that's only a guess. It may be he still wants to finish what he started."

77

"I'm of the same mind. Could you spare a few more days?"

The Vaquero sighed in irritation, and did not reply.

"I'll pay you, a few days' wages. It's no bounty, but it's what I can do."

"What do you have in mind?"

"Stay with Elanor at her place. You and Johnny. At least until the funeral. The town will be on edge, I'll need to be here."

"And when I leave?"

"I'll have Johnny stay with her longer. But I'd feel safer with you there for now. At least for a little while. I figure if he's going to strike again, it will be soon."

The Vaquero thought this over. "Alright. I'll stay until the husband is buried, then I'm riding on."

"Thank you, Vaquero." The Sheriff sounded truly grateful. The Vaquero tipped his hat.

He spent the next three days holed up at the Slater Farm with Elanor and Deputy Johnny. Those three days were mostly uneventful. Elanor kept to herself, but expressed gratitude to both men for their kindness. Still in a lot of pain, she slept a good portion of the time. Johnny and The Vaquero played a lot of checkers. The Vaquero enjoyed Johnny's youthful spirit. When Elanor was sleeping, he would quietly tell Johnny of some of his adventures and the boy gobbled up every word.

At the start of the third day, they had run out of water. The Vaquero grabbed two empty buckets and made his way to the well. It sat about fifty yards behind the house and close to a line of trees. The woods behind the tree line were thick, and it did not escape him how easily a man could hide in them.

Before The Vaquero started the pump to fill his first bucket, he got the distinct sense of being watched. A cowboy's intuition. His hand smoothly slid down and grabbed the handle of his revolver. From the woods, a slow southern voice spoke to him.

"You pull that gun out and I'll shoot you dead where you stand, dark-skin."

"Wesley Nelson. I thought you'd be around here somewhere."

There was a long pause. Surprise maybe, that this cowboy knew his name. "Pretty famous aren't I?"

"I don't know if I'd say that."

"Who are you?"

"I'm a bounty hunter."

"Well, I'll be damned. What's a famous killer like me got a bounty at these days?"

"It's pretty small. Not big enough that I've bothered chasing after you."

"You're lying." Wesley sounded genuinely offended. "You're chasing me now."

"You're right. I am now. But not for the bounty. I've taken a personal interest in you." The Vaquero walked his eyes discreetly down the tree line, trying to get a visual on Wesley.

"You won't be chasing after me if I shoot you."

The Vaquero pondered this risk. "Something tells me you don't have a gun, Wesley. And even if you did, I don't know if you'd land that first shot. You see, I'm pretty quick with this pistol. And I don't miss my shots."

Wesley answered with the distinct cocking sound of a gun. "You irritate me, cowboy."

"Good." The Vaquero's eyes caught a small piece of fabric fluttering behind a large tree. He was certain Wesley was there. But the line of sight and potential shot was less than ideal.

"I have decided that I am going to allow Elanor to live, for now. I have other business to attend to."

"That's a good decision."

"Before I move on, though. I want to hear you say that."

"Say what?"

"That I am allowing Elanor to live."

The Vaquero was tempted to contest the point, but thought it was best not to prod the conflict. "You've shown great mercy, Wesley."

"Yes, I have. I'll visit her again one day. But for now, she's safe. I'd suggest you don't follow me."

"I will follow you, Wesley. It's what I do."

"I won't show you mercy, dark-skin."

"I wouldn't expect you to." With those final words, The Vaquero heard the sound of retreating steps. He considered shooting, or at least pursuing, but he felt the odds favored him poorly if he did so. And he did believe that Wesley would now leave the area. Despite this, he felt confident he would catch up to Wesley in time.

The Vaquero never told the Deputy or Sheriff Downy of his encounter with Wesley in the woods. He simply expressed his confidence that the murderer had moved on. After the funeral of David Slater and several heartfelt moments of appreciation, The

Vaquero rode on in pursuit of a new bounty ticket. Wesley Nelson, wanted dead or alive, with a $1000 reward. On September 6th, 1898, The Vaquero would catch up with Wesley in Fateville, Arkansas.

3

In Pursuit

After Elanor Slater slipped through his fingers, Wesley Nelson spent four long and frustrating days in the Iowa woods. He watched from afar as two young men came and cleaned up his mess. He was amused as they struggled at first to uncover David's corpse from the pile of firewood, and then to carry the fat fuck into a wagon.

He was pleased when Elanor returned to the farmhouse, but disappointed to see her in the company of two men. One of them was from the initial cleanup crew. A deputy, most likely. But the other man, he was a new addition and something different.

The second man wasn't particularly tall, but he looked strong and battle tested. He wore dark pants and a long white sleeve shirt that buttoned up the middle. He'd often wear a coat, even in the heat of the day. It was dark brown and appeared to be leather, possibly suede. There was also the cowboy hat. It was large brimmed and dark, like the man's skin. On most men, the hat would have seemed too large, cartoonish even. But on this man, it all balanced. This cowboy only carried one revolver. It also looked cartoonishly large. It hung in a holster by his right hip.

Wesley feared no man. But he was smart enough to be cautious around this cowboy. There was something unusual about him. He was a different breed.

After four days of tireless waiting and watching, Wesley's food supplies were getting low. He knew he'd need to move on soon. He packed up his camp and paid one more visit to the farmhouse. He'd only made it as far as the water well when he spotted the cowboy alone. He didn't intend to have a confrontation, only to watch. But the cowboy seemed to pick up on Wesley's presence and reached for his revolver. Wesley thought his best play was to call the cowboy's bluff. For the most part, he was right.

The two men exchanged some words, then went their separate ways. Wesley retrieved his things and instead of working further north, he made his way back south into Missouri.

He kept his routine of moving from town to town, looking for work as a carpenter, all the while looking for new victims. But now he had several things working against him. He wasn't famous, as he liked to think, but he was certainly more apt to get recognized. He started cutting his hair shorter and keeping his face clean shaven whenever he could. It was a much different look than the wild-eyed, and wiry-haired man in the wanted posters.

There was also the problem of the cowboy. He was always close behind. Somewhere along the way, Wesley picked up that folks called this man The Vaquero. He believed it meant cowboy in Spanish. He didn't understand the nickname, as The Vaquero was clearly a black man. He also understood this man was a bounty hunter and one with a reputation for being relentless.

In Jefferson City, Missouri, The Vaquero almost caught up with Wesley. He had stayed working at the same place too long, a general store named Lee's. Wesley knew he should have left sooner, if it wasn't for that fact that Lee had a daughter. A pretty one. And Wesley wanted to get to know her a little better. But the goddamn Vaquero was in town and asking questions. Wesley chose to ride out before the bounty hunter could locate him.

He had made off with nothing but a few day's pay and some trashy monster magazines that Lee hid behind the counter. One issue in particular grabbed his attention. It was titled *The Grim Reaper Cometh!* This particular depiction of the Grim Reaper, a dark-robed skeleton with demonic red eyes, had an appetite for scantily dressed young women.

He was pursued by The Vaquero for over a year. And during that time he didn't manage to commit a single murder. The Vaquero, in relentless pursuit, never allowed him the time to settle in and kill.

In June 1898, Wesley found himself in Fateville, Arkansas, where he got hired on at a local furniture store. He believed his trip further south into Arkansas had finally shaken The Vaquero off his trail. So he settled in. He got comfortable. And the familiar obsessions reared up again. This time, the wife of the furniture store owner drew his attention. Witches visited Wesley in his dreams and demanded blood. He promised to provide.

***

The Vaquero was not shaken from Wesley's trail. But after a year of hunting, he knew he'd need to change his approach. When Wesley crossed into Arkansas, The Vaquero thought this would be the opportune time. He narrowed Wesley down to two or three small towns all in a twenty five mile radius. Then he pulled back and waited. He cashed in on some small-time local tickets and gave Wesley plenty of space to breathe. And time to get comfortable.

The Vaquero didn't want to give him enough time to kill. Although he knew that was something that could happen at any time. But he knew to catch Wesley, he'd need him to slow down. To feel as though he didn't need to run so fast. When he felt enough time had passed, then he'd move in. He'd ask questions fast and be discreet. Then he'd find that son of a bitch and bring him in. Cold.

The Vaquero's plan worked, mostly. But when he paid a visit to Henry Colton, owner of Colton's Furniture, he found Wesley Nelson much sooner than he expected.

There was talk that he might be working at Colton's Furniture under a false name. The tip was solid and from a good source. The Vaquero didn't want to pop into the furniture store and start asking questions. If his timing wasn't right, Wesley might get wind and start running again. He decided to stop by the owner's house late in the evening and ask some questions away from watchful eyes.

But as The Vaquero approached Henry Colton's home, he heard gunfire. He raced into the house and found Wesley Nelson naked, clubbing a woman on the head with the butt of his revolver. There was another man, presumably Henry, lying on the ground with a large knife plunged into his chest. He also appeared to be shot. A thick pool of dark blood was forming around his head.

The Vaquero processed all this with a hunter's speed. He took it all in, but wasn't distracted by it. His focus remained on Wesley and completing the goal. He raised his cartoonishly large revolver and took aim at the Missouri Mauler.

Then something happened that in twenty-five years of bounty hunting had never happened to The Vaquero before. His pistol jammed. His gun was cleaned meticulously on a daily basis. It was an almost ritualistic behavior. So when his squeezing trigger finger felt no give, he simply couldn't process what was happening. His hunter's instincts, in that brief moment, failed him. Wesley seized the opportunity and shot The Vaquero in the head. Luckily, it was not a direct hit. The slug scraped the side of The Vaquero's skull and rattled his brain, but fortunately didn't spill out any grey matter.

The Vaquero came to, probably awakened by the screaming woman tied to the bed, and was surprised to find himself alive. The right side of his head felt like it had been bucked by a horse. He touched the side of his face and saw his hand was covered in blood. How long had he been out? Was there still time?

He crawled his way over to the dead man on the floor and placed two bloody fingers on his neck. There was no pulse. He placed his left ear, probably the only ear that could still hear anything, close to the man's mouth. There was no breath. He then grasped the handle of the large knife sticking from the man's chest and yanked it out with a swift upward motion.

He stood up, dizzy and confused, but able to keep his balance. He cut the ties that bound the screaming woman to the bed. He then turned and followed a trail of bloody footprints out of the room. He saw his pistol as he exited, but he felt betrayed by it, and chose to leave it behind. If he caught Wesley, the knife would be a more personal way to end things. He ran out into the night, his head darting both ways until he located his target. Wesley appeared to be injured and hadn't gotten far. The Vaquero sprinted after him, closing to within several paces of him on the street. He could hear footsteps behind him, could see lights flashing above him, but he remained focused on his mark.

***

Wesley heard steps behind him and turned to find The Vaquero closing in on him. He raised his pistol, but heard a gunshot before he could pull the trigger. And then, blackness.

He suddenly found himself in the Iowa woods, camped beside a dying fire. Green witch eyes glowed all around him through the trees. Those eyes demanded blood and he hadn't delivered on his promise.

He was sure the witches would move in. He was sure they would devour him. They would revoke his Warlock powers and damn his soul to hell. But above him, what did he see? Lights? Brilliant glowing orbs shined through the canopy of trees. It was though there were a hundred moons filling the sky. And these lights were good. They wanted him. They would save him. The beams illuminated him, basking him in a majestic white luminescence. The blackness was gone, all he could see was light.

4
A Garden Where It Shouldn't Grow

The Vaquero was sitting by a small creek. The water was still and dark. The creek seemed to run a great length in one direction, while the other direction disappeared into a hillside. His clothes were damp, as though he'd been in the creek and was drying out.

"Open your eyes. I think you've rested enough." The Vaquero was startled by the child's voice behind him. He turned to see a young man, maybe eleven or twelve years old. He was standing in his underwear, and his skin was deathly white.

"Who are you? Where is this place?"

"It's just a place." The boy's pink lips were tinged with blue. The Vaquero realized the boy didn't look cold. He looked dead. "I said open your eyes."

The Vaquero opened his eyes. He was in a small, plain room, lying in a bed and covered with a thin white blanket. The left side of his head throbbed, causing the room to swim in and out of focus. He blinked a couple of times, and saw his ten brown toes jutting up from under the blanket. He looked up, and saw a smooth brown crucifix hanging on the wall ahead of him.

In the corner of the room, lightly sleeping in what must be an extremely uncomfortable chair, was the unbelievably beautiful woman from the Colton house. Her face was bruised and swollen. Her sandy brown hair fell down over her features. Her hair looked clean but tangled. She looked wounded and tired. But through it all, what an amazing sight she was.

The Vaquero's heart steadily increased its pace. His chest moved up and down, trying to take in normal breaths, shallow at first, then deeper and deeper. He tried to speak, but realized he could not. Come to think of it, he could not move at all. It was like his brain woke up before the rest of his body. He calmed an inner tidal wave of panic and focused on his breathing. He then tried to wiggle his toes and was pleased to see ten brown piggies dancing at the end of the bed. Tingles moved up through his body and all the machinery started to wake up.

"Miss Colton?" The Vaquero's voice sounded stronger than he had anticipated.

Susan's eyes opened and The Vaquero was stunned by their deep amber tone. He had seen this woman. Hell, he'd seen her naked. He had cut her loose from her own bed. But he was shot, and his blood was hot at the time. He hadn't truly seen her. She was breath-taking.

Susan jumped to her feet. She cringed and grabbed at the small of her back. Her eyes shot daggers at the chair. Then she smiled, embarrassingly. "I don't know your name, sir," she said, working her way across the room to his bedside.

"People call me Vaquero." An icepick plunged through the side of The Vaquero's brain and sent envoys of pain through his body. He grabbed at the side of his head.

"Don't talk if it hurts." She sat down on the bed and lightly stroked the other side of his face. Her touch felt medicinal. His hand patted at the thick bandages on the side of his head.

"It's fine," he said, lowering his hand back down to his side.

"What kind of name is that, Vaquero?"

"It's Spanish."

"I took you for a black man. Are you Spanish?"

"No, ma'am. Just a name some Mexican friends gave me. Long, long time ago."

"You saved my life. Do you know that, Vaquero?"

"I remember. I'm sorry I wasn't there sooner. I could have saved you both."

Susan dropped her eyes and pulled her hand back. "I wish so too. Henry, my husband, he saved my life. Both of you did."

"They had a gunfight. Your husband and Wesley. That's the gunfire I heard outside." The sequence of events was getting clearer in The Vaquero's mind.

"Wesley? Is that his real name?"

"Yes. Wesley Nelson."

"I knew him as Weston. He worked for my husband."

"He was a wanted man. Killed a lot of folks all over these parts. I'd been on his trail for a little over a year now."

"Why were you chasing him? Are you a lawman?"

"Not quite. Just a bounty hunter."

"*Just* a bounty hunter? That's no small thing."

"No big thing either. Most people find something they are good at. For some reason, that's the gift God gave me." His eyes looked up at the crucifix and he briefly wondered if he truly believed in God.

"I don't know if you'll get the bounty."

"I don't deserve it. You do."

Susan looked deep into The Vaquero's eyes. "I'm glad I was the one who put him down."

"It's not an easy thing, killing a man. But some men deserve it more than most. Wesley Nelson certainly did."

Susan seemed briefly lost in her thoughts, then she reset. "They couldn't find his body."

"What?"

"It was gone. When the Sheriff and his deputies arrived, it wasn't there. You and I were both unconscious. They were able to wake me up, but you've been asleep since. That was two days ago."

The Vaquero thought all this over. "I know dead. He was dead. You put him down."

"I know I did too. But, I can't say what happened after that."

"People do all kinds of strange things. Maybe someone saw an opportunity, ran off with the body. No one's tried to cash in?"

"I don't think anyone even knows who he is. The Sheriff keeps coming by, hoping you'll wake up and fill us in on all the details."

"How bad is it?" The Vaquero, suddenly remembering the thick bandages on his head, patted at them some more.

Susan's hand reached out to grab his arm and gently pulled it away. "Stop that."

"Yes, ma'am."

"You were shot in the head, Vaquero. But the doctor said the bullet didn't go through your skull. He said it bounced off it. It took a big chunk of your skin with it and..." She paused to clear her throat. "...And the top part of your ear."

"I didn't need that part of my ear." He smiled at her, and saw Susan's eyes light up. She looked away, running a hand through her hair.

"When you are able to leave here. Where will you go?"

The Vaquero thought this over. "I don't know. Been chasing that man for so long now, that's about all I've thought about. Guess I could get my mind thinking about other things." Those last words felt flirtatious, and he was instantly struck by guilt.

"You'll need some time to heal."

"Yes, reckon I will."

"If I asked you something, would you not think poorly of me?"

"I don't know you very well...but..." The Vaquero trailed off in his thoughts.

"What is it?"

"I just realized I don't know your first name."

"Susan. Unless you want to keep on calling me ma'am or Miss Colton?"

The Vaquero chuckled. "No ma'am. I like Susan. And I don't know you very well, but I don't think I could think poorly of you. You saved my life too, you know?"

"Stay with me."

"Pardon?" Her remark caught The Vaquero off guard.

"Just for a while. While you rest and heal. You make me feel safe."

"People may talk, with your husband being gone and all."

"Let them talk. I want to feel safe. And I want to watch you get better." Again, she gazed deeply into The Vaquero's dark green eyes. "If you don't want to—"

The Vaquero reached out and grasped her hand. His touch wasn't entirely platonic, but it was respectful and gracious. "I'd be honored, Susan, if you'd have me. I'll warn you though, I like to eat. Might eat you out of house and home."

Now it was Susan's turn to chuckle. "I like to cook. And I think I can afford you for a little while."

***

The Sheriff would come and be pleasantly surprised to find out The Vaquero was awake. The Vaquero would go on to explain who he was and also reveal the identity of Henry's killer. He knew the Sheriff would look into his background and would find a bounty hunter of prestigious reputation, but with no body of the killer, The Vaquero wondered if he might himself fall under suspicion. Luckily, two repairmen working a fence line had seen The Vaquero and Susan chasing Wesley down the street. They had also seen Susan shoot him dead. Their recollection after that was also missing.

Once the Sheriff knew the identity of the killer, he sent word to a U.S. Marshall in Small Rock, Arkansas. The Marshall rode in and also spoke to all involved. It was his judgement, as well as the Sheriff's that Wesley Nelson was indeed dead. But with no body, he would not be able to pay out on a bounty. He gave Susan $100 that he told her was from a victim's fund. The Vaquero got a handshake and some words of admiration.

Truth be told, Susan wouldn't need the $100 from the victim's fund. Henry was well insured and she collected $7,500 due to his untimely death. She was also now the sole owner of Colton's Furniture, which she sold for another $7,500. All this on top of

Henry's considerable savings and Susan was sitting comfortably with $20,000 in the bank. That may not be enough to get her through the rest of her life, but she'd be able to pay off her house and do okay for the next several years.

The house, and the ten acres it sat on, she'd likely sell down the road. The thought of being in that home alone, ever again, terrified her. But for a while at least, The Vaquero would be there, and she'd feel safe. As it turned out, her heart would grow to feel more than just safe.

Several months had passed since The Vaquero woke up in a small hospital room. He now spent his mornings waking up in Susan's former bedroom. She couldn't bring herself to stay in that room, so she had moved into the guest room. The Vaquero would often wake to the smell of sizzling meat and strong black coffee.

They took good care of each other. He had some rough days where the pain was unbearable. She had a lot of rough nights where the nightmares were equally bad. They got each other through both. She'd forgive him when his head would ache and his words would seem short and cross. He showed patience when she'd wake in the night, screaming and beating on him until he could finally calm her down. On each of their darkest days, they filled it with the light of the other.

Through all this, they kept deeper feelings at bay.

One morning, Susan awoke to discover The Vaquero was not in his bed. He had awakened well before her. She found him standing in the backyard of her home, pointing his gun into the field. About twenty-five yards out, he had set a glass bottle on an old tree stump. She watched for some time at the window, expecting to hear an eventual gunshot. But it never came. He just stood there, aiming but never firing.

"Are you okay?" she said, walking up softly behind him. Her feet were bare and it felt good to walk on the cool, wet grass.

"No. Reckon I'm not." He dropped the gun and turned to her. "When I aimed my pistol at Wesley, I had the drop on him. I always get the drop on my tickets. And I never miss. But my gun jammed. Then..." The Vaquero feigned a shot to his own head.

"And?"

"And my gun doesn't jam. I take better care of this thing than I do myself." He rested the gun in the palms of his hands and admired it. "This beautiful gun didn't jam. I did. I don't think my finger ever pulled the trigger."

Susan got close to The Vaquero and looked up into his eyes. "What does it matter?"

"I don't know." He shook his head. "I came out here to shoot and my finger won't work. My hands feel like they don't belong to me. I thought maybe it was from taking a bullet to the skull, like maybe it scrambled my brain. Broke things about me. But then I started thinking back to that night. I think I was broken already."

Susan took the gun and placed it gently on the ground. "Would you make love to me?" She pressed her body against him and opened the front of her satin robe.

The Vaquero hesitated, only for a moment, before lifting her up. She was light and felt good in his arms as she wrapped her legs around his waist. The air seemed to fill with that same energy that comes before a lightning strike.

"My heart has longed for you since I woke up and saw you in the hospital. I questioned my belief in God that morning, but you were there like one of his angels." His words grabbed for her, but his face still showed reluctance.

She lightly kissed his lips. "Then what is stopping you?"

"Will you feel wrong for this later?"

"I don't think you and I can be together, truly together, for a while maybe. Maybe never. We both still have healing to do. I loved my husband. And I know I shouldn't feel anything for another man yet. The earth of my heart should be dead trees and salted soil. But there is a garden there. A garden where it should not grow. And that garden is you." Tears were dripping from her eyes and The Vaquero wiped them away with a free hand.

Then lightning struck in the form of a passionate kiss. They both had a feeling of breaking free from heavy chains. The warmth of her loins pressed against his stomach, and she nibbled at the scarred remains of his left ear. He turned and started to carry her into the house.

"No," she cried. "Right here. Please, right here. Not in that house." And so it was right there, they made love in the cool wet grass.

A week later The Vaquero would ride out. He didn't know if he was still a bounty hunter. Hell, he didn't even know if he could fire his gun. But he would go back to the road as long as needed, for Susan and himself to mend all the broken parts of their minds. Then maybe, just maybe, they would come together again someday.

"I won't live here, in this house, if you ever return. Will you find me?" Susan asked, adoring The Vaquero's muscular silhouette, sitting high on his horse against the backdrop of a rising sun.

"I'll find you. Finding people is one thing I'm rather good at." Those were the last words The Vaquero would speak to Susan for ten long years.

5

This Ain't God's Work

Following the brutal murder of his entire family, John spent the next several nights sleeping in his office at Robinson Bank and Trust. After investigating the carnage, the Sheriff had made arrangements to get everything in John's house cleaned up. His boys would spend days collecting body parts, scrubbing blood off walls, and burning items that couldn't be cleaned in a fire pit behind the home.

The remains of his daughters and wife were gathered and removed from the Robinson family home. The little that was left of them had to be hauled away in canvas sacks to the local mortuary and funeral home. It was a psychologically damaging event to all the men who helped clean up the house, but luckily one they would soon enough forget.

The bank continued to operate while John holed up in his office. No one disturbed him. He slept. He drank. Mostly drank. He contemplated suicide on several occasions, even once holding his pistol, with the beautifully inscribed handle (R-O-B-I-N-S-O-N), deep inside his mouth. But the thought of vengeance and justice kept pulling him back.

He wondered briefly if suspicion would fall u
had two alibis, sure. It would not be contested that h
at the saloon late into the night. But did he go home
slaughter his family in a drunken rage? He didn't thir...
would draw this conclusion, but it wasn't impossible. If he found his
way into a hangman's noose, what of justice then? At least it would
be a welcome end to the pain.

More than anything over those few days in the office, John
felt dirty. He was dirty in the physical sense, but this was more of a
mental feeling. What had spoken to him in his head? And didn't it
leave some kind of trail behind? Like a snail's slime or a rotten
aftertaste. Whatever it was, it lingered. What was the disgusting
creature that John had pursued that night and why couldn't he see
its face?

When the bloody work of cleaning up John's house was
done, he returned home. In a zombie-like state, he bathed himself.
He ate some stale bread. He drank more whiskey. His mattress had
been burned behind the house, leaving only an empty bedframe. So
the first night he slept on Mary Ellen's bed. It still smelled like her.
That brought him a strange mixture of joy and grief. He cried
through the night, sleeping very little.

The day of the funeral he managed to get himself dressed
and presentable. For a man that generally looked well put together,
he now looked unkempt and rugged. He was oblivious to this
change, nor would he have cared. He made his way into town and
to the local church, where most of the townsfolk had gathered to
pay their respects.

There were three caskets at the front of the church. All
three were small, but two were even smaller and John presumed
those belonged to his daughters. Each lid was closed. John imagined
that anything left of his family was in bags under the closed coffin
lids. Should he have seen to it they were burned? He didn't know.
As final as everything was, burning them would feel even more final.

"Thank you all for coming here today. Such a large crowd."
The preacher was a tall, thin man. He was young, even handsome,

despite a pair of thick glasses and a receding hairline. "It's such a large crowd because the family we honor today is so respected. Those who have passed. And those who are still living." The preacher looked towards John who kept his head down, hearing the kind words, but unable to acknowledge.

"Let us pray." The congregation all lowered their heads. "The Lord is my light and my salvation; whom shall I fear? *The Adversary.* The Lord is the strength of my life; of whom shall I be afraid? *The Adversary.* Though a host should encamp against me, my heart shall not fear. Though war should rise up against me, in this will I be confident. One thing have I desired of the Lord, that will I seek after. That I may dwell in the house of the Lord all the days of my life. To behold the beauty of the Lord, and to inquire in his temple. For in the time of trouble he shall hide me in his pavilion. In the secret of his tabernacle shall he hide me. He shall set me up upon a rock. Amen." The congregation echoed in unison. *Amen.*

John's grief weighed him down. He felt smothered in it. But he could still be brave. He had shown bravery his entire life. Hadn't he been brave exploring that dark Missouri cave? Hadn't he been brave carrying his brother through a murderous horde of bees? Hadn't he been brave learning to forgive himself for not saving his brother's life? Did he forgive himself? Calling up all his strength and courage, John raised himself up on the pew. He sat straight, not crying, and held his eyes up to meet the room.

"Sometimes we question the Lord. We question our faith in the Lord," the preacher continued. It was August, and sweating in a church at this time of year wasn't unusual. But the day had been overcast. The temperature in the hall was pleasant. So why was the preacher sweating so profusely? John stared curiously, and then all at once felt guilty for allowing it to distract him from his grief.

He was about to chalk it up to nervousness. It must be hard, speaking to such a large crowd about such an emotional circumstance. But as he looked around, many people were sweating. He felt as cool as could be. Was something wrong with him? Or was something wrong with all of them?

"It is not our place to question God's plan..." Globs of sweat popped out of the preacher's balding head and ran down his face in streams. His white collar was starting to yellow.

This was strange. And what was it he heard some people whispering during the prayer? John had never known, and would never know, such technology as a VCR, but he was now hitting a mental rewind <<< button. Whom shall I fear?...*Something*. Whom shall I be afraid?...*Something*. He was being ridiculous. They must have said amen.

"I didn't know John's family personally. But I've heard so many delightful things about them. About the joy they brought to our town."

John needed to focus, but the room was shrinking. Everyone but him seemed to be sweating like pigs. Some of them were whispering. He could smell something like dead leaves. For a gut-churning moment, he imagined the smell was from his family's remains in the coffins. But that was also ridiculous. He had been so disengaged during the entire process; he didn't even know if their remains were in the coffins. What had he done in the past week other than drink and write a check for the funeral? He wasn't brave. He was a coward.

"Disease does not discriminate. It takes those we love. Those we hate."

Disease? What was he talking about? Is murder a disease?

"But the fever that took these beautiful lives could not sicken their souls. For the Lord breaks all fevers. Let us pray once more."

Disease? Fever? *They were cut into a thousand pieces, you fuck.* John realized the line between his thoughts and what he said out loud was becoming increasingly thin.

"Behold, I tell you a mystery. We shall not all fall asleep, but we will all be changed, in an instant, in the blink of an eye, at the last trumpet. For the trumpet will sound, the dead will be raised incorruptible, and we shall be changed..." The preacher continued on and closed out the services. A room full of townsfolk paid their respects, patted at their sweating foreheads, and offered John their condolences. Most of those who attended the funeral also followed in procession to the Harrison Cemetery. On a cool and overcast day in August, John Robinson laid his young family to rest.

Long after the last shovels of dirt had filled in three adjacent holes, John still stood at the graveside. It was starting to sprinkle and the cool water felt good on his skin. Beside him stood a good friend. A drinking buddy, yes. But also a good friend. And both men were sober as they stood at the graves.

"This ain't God's work you know?" Dodd placed a shaking hand on John's shoulder.

"I know, Dodd. We all have free will, I believe that." John turned to look at Dodd and found him more visibly distraught than he was. "The pistol you made me..."

Dodd took his hand off John's shoulder and wiped at his nose. "What about it?"

"That night, it was the only weapon I had. The only thing on my side. It brought me comfort."

Dodd looked confused. "The night your family died?"

101

"Yes."

"I guess I don't understand, John."

"What don't you understand, Dodd, tell me?"

"Why did a gun help you? Not as though you can shoot away sickness."

John stared in silence for a moment. "Who was sick, Dodd?"

Dodd's face had started to shake. His complexion was turning bright red. And was he sweating? Or were those the first drops of real rain? "Your family was sick. All of 'ems."

John felt angry at first, then puzzled, and then concerned. Dodd's face looked like it was going to split in two. He looked like a man trying to have two different conversations at the same time. "How did my family die, Dodd?"

"F-F-F-Fever. They all caught a fever. Took 'em fast. Ain't God's work they got sick. But it's his mercy they went fast." Dodd was definitely sweating. He was crying now, too. Not from grief, but from something else.

John thought about pressing on, but decided any further questions might drive his good friend insane. "God's mercy. Amen. Thank you, Dodd." John placed his hand on Dodd's shoulder. The two men left the cemetery together and went their separate ways.

John didn't drink that night. Nor did he sleep. He'd need to be in town at first light and meet with the Sheriff.

Sheriff Armstrong was a driven man. His work was his life. He had never settled down or had children. Never having kids of his own, he couldn't fully relate to the pain John Robinson was experiencing. Yet still, his heart ached. To lose them all. So unexpectedly. So quickly. What a kick in the teeth life can give a man.

They sat inside the small, one-room Sheriff station, on opposite sides of a large desk. The desk was a magnificently polished wood that seemed almost out of place in the rustic room. Tension rested comfortably on the silence.

"What can I look into for you, John?" The Sheriff's tone was sincere.

"Oh hell, I don't know. Are we going to catch the man who did this?" John's tone, on the other hand, was sarcastic and confrontational.

"I don't mean to upset you, John. I can't even imagine what you are going through. But what man? Who did what?"

"My family was taken from me. Murdered. Why is everyone acting so goddamn oblivious to that?"

"It may feel like it, John, but getting sick isn't murder. It's not something we can control."

"Either this town is losing its fucking mind or I am." John stood up and turned away, now sounding more beaten down than angry.

The first beads of sweat started to birth on the Sherriff's forehead. "No one is losing their mind, John. This is just hard. You might want to see the doc. Just to be safe."

"You're shaking."

"Pardon?" The Sheriff wiped his brow.

"You're shaking. And sweating like a pig. You coming down with something?"

"No, no. It's just. It's hot in here."

"Three people die of a fever overnight. Might mean there's something bad going around. Something that might be dangerous

103

for the whole town." The Sheriff was a tough man, but John's gaze at that moment could cut through steel. It was cutting right through the Sheriff.

He wiped his brow again with a shaky hand and scrunched his face in a confused knot. John had that same feeling as he did with Dodd. As though he needed to stop. To pull back. To let this go. "I'm sorry, Sheriff, for losing my temper. I just haven't been thinking clearly. You enjoy the rest of your day."

The Sheriff's appearance made an abrupt improvement. "Thank You, John. You take care now."

John stepped out into the street and walked over to his horse, Carl. He gently stroked Carl's side and tried to make sense of everything. "Something isn't right here, Carl. Whoever, whatever, took them from us. I think part of it is still here. It hangs over this town like a cloud." Carl gave his familiar, silent agreement. "Where do we go from here? What do we do?"

Later John found himself going through the double doors of the saloon and sitting at the bar. There was a piano player that night. He was good. He played differently. Faster than most. John was two shots in when the piano man played a song he had never heard before.

"Gon' head on up to Kansas City. Kansas City, is where I run." The piano player sang as his fingers danced on the keys. John watched and listened, feeling hypnotized. "I hear the girls in Kansas City, they like to have a lot of fun." A terrible realization occurred to him, that *something* was going to Kansas City and nothing about it would be fun. John paid his tab and hurriedly left the bar.

***

Two weeks later, Dodd Stevens received a message summoning him to the Robinson Bank and Trust. Upon arriving, he was met by a short, bespectacled man wearing a fine suit. He waved Dodd into John's office.

"Please, please sit down."

"Where is John, I mean, Mr. Robinson? This is his office."

"Well, it's no longer his office. And I'd also add I think he's okay with you calling him John."

Dodd fumbled his fingers through his disheveled red hair. "I don't understand."

"Allow me to explain. My name is Harlan Epping." The short man extended his hand and the two men shook. "I represent William Fargo. He owns a bank that competes with John. Competes with Robinson Bank and Trust." Harlan raised his arms as if to showcase the room around him.

"Why are you here, Mr. Epping?"

"Your friend John sold us his bank. We paid him a good deal, but he needed the money fast and so his price was fair."

"Where is John?"

"He left town. I'm not sure where. I understand he suffered a great tragedy. I imagine he just needed a change. A fresh start. Maybe a simpler life."

Dodd was saddened by this news. He was sad that he may never see John again. He was also a little hurt that he didn't tell him goodbye. "Why did you bring me here to tell me all this? Who am I to you?"

"John asked us to. Part of the deal."

"Well, thank you, I guess." Dodd turned to leave.

"Wait." Harlan was grinning. "That's not all, Mr. Stevens." Harlan retrieved a letter from what was formerly John's desk and held it out. Dodd hesitated, then snatched it from the man's hand. He stared at it curiously and saw it was addressed to himself. "Take no offense please, but...can you read, Mr. Stevens?"

"I can read goddamn it," Dodd said as he peeled at the letter's sealing.

"There is something I need to inform you of before you read the letter."

Dodd paused. "Go on."

"With the money John received from the sale of the bank, he kept some in a personal account. He also took a great deal. Another portion was used to pay off the remaining note on his home. And yet another portion was deposited into your account."

"My account?"

"Yes, your account." Harlan seemed genuinely delighted to be giving good news.

"How much was this portion?"

"$5,000."

Feelings swirled in Dodd like a tornado. He felt joy, gratitude, and sorrow. He also felt scared. Scared of how he'd handle so much money. "I've never had that much money before." Dodd wiped a tear from his eye.

"One last thing, then I'll leave you to your letter." Harlan pulled another piece of paper from John's former desk. "This is a deed to your new home. John signed it over to you." A few tears now became many. Dodd's knees buckled and started to collapse. Harlan darted around the desk and helped keep Dodd on his feet. "Easy now. Why don't you sit?"

"That's a good idea." Dodd sunk down into a cushioned brown armchair. He placed the deed onto the desk and proceeded to open his letter.

To my friend Dodd,

By the time you are reading this, you should know that I've left you some money and I've signed over my house to you. I'm sorry I wasn't able to tell you goodbye. The money, or the house, won't make up for that. But I hope it buys me some forgiveness. Since the death of my family, I feel called to the road. I don't know that I can ever come back here. But I do hope to see you again. I've never been good at writing a lot of words. Just know that I consider you my best friend and I want nothing but the best for you. Don't spend too much of the money on whiskey. I mean it. And maybe take some of the money and get away for a little while. There's something not right in town. I'd let the air clear out for a bit. Alright, friend, that's all the words I've got.

John

John would never see his friend Dodd again. But he'd be happy to know that Dodd did well the rest of his days. And though he would never believe it, Dodd never touched a drop of whiskey again.

John was now a traveler of the road. He didn't consider himself a cowboy. He considered himself a hunter. He left first for Kansas City. And the more miles he put between himself and Harrison, the clearer his purpose became. He had the scent of his prey, and he was in pursuit. Hundreds of miles, hundreds of nightmares, all lay ahead. And despite his good advice to Dodd, lots of whiskey lay ahead too.

6

The Adversary

You are doing well, brave reader. Up to this point, you've endured some truly awful things. You've seen men at their worst and most despicable. And while it's less common throughout the universe, (mankind truly is terrible) men are not the only creatures to commit hideous acts. One such creature I will tell you about now.

Things get a bit complicated when trying to describe to you a creature, completely alien to yourself. Its physical body, mental processes, and even the world around it all exist in a way your brain simply won't be able to comprehend. So you'll need to forgive me if I've dumbed things down a bit for you. I've done my best to translate what can't truly be translated.

Here we look upon Glenn. Interstellar traveler and researcher from the planet Verota. Glenn has been assigned to the planet Earth for observation and specimen collection. He arrived on Earth and began his research in December 1897.

Glenn does not come from a civilization of hierarchy. His position, his purpose, is special, but all beings of Glenn's species are special. All roles and functions are sacred. Individual needs are not considered over the needs of the species.

Glenn's race of beings, we'll call them husks, are flesh and blood. But they do not have a central brain. Their brain is part of their entire physical body. They are a uniquely thought-based species. Their bodies, a shape-shifting, jelly-like husk, are directly influenced by their conscious manipulation.

Husks can communicate telepathically with most creatures and they gain nourishment through telepathic absorption. Thousands of years prior, husks found a way to absorb the complete consciousness of other beings. This ultimate nourishment accelerated their mental capacity and physical development. It was a monumental achievement for their species, expanding their prominence across the galaxy.

They quickly discovered there was only one risk with this newly found technology and evolution. The telepathic absorption, feeding if you will, of low-intelligence beings caused no adverse reactions. But when the husks attempted to completely absorb the consciousness of intelligent beings, the results were catastrophic. It led to madness and ultimately the death of the host.

Millions of husks, Glenn included, were sent out into the galaxy to gather countless specimens of life with telepathic substance. Specimens are researched, analyzed, and catalogued, with the hope that someday all creatures can be consciously devoured and take their species into an even more advanced state of evolution.

Glenn's mission on Earth would be no different. He knew of human beings. He had learned of them from previous visit archives. They were peculiar. Apt to violence. And he liked that.

He was a little different from most husks. He had some feelings that weren't acceptable. While in Verota, he had to conceal those parts of himself, which was no easy task in a world of telepathic creatures. But while on the mission, it was only himself, the ship, and his specimens. There were no prying eyes, or prying thoughts, for that matter.

Glenn's ultimate destination was Earth, but there were plenty of stops to be made along the way. He collected many creatures, off the books, if you will. He found he enjoyed inflicting creatures with physical pain. There was a beauty in watching living things suffer. He didn't understand this part of himself, but he knew he enjoyed it.

He always associated his feelings of violence with sex. Sexual production in his species was no longer a physical act, but more of a laboratory controlled task. Still, he felt some ancient connection to sex, from a time when it still meant physical and psychological conjoining. Or as he would often fantasize, physical and psychological domination.

It was September 6, 1898, when Glenn arrived in Fateville, Arkansas. His spaceship, a physical thing, but also telepathic in nature, had finished its process of cycling down. When visiting the civilization hubs of intelligent creatures, procedures were to emit a strong telepathic presence on the local population. This would lead to an amnesiac effect, causing the inhabitants to be ignorant of the visitation.

A frequent side effect of the ship's telepathic overload was the observation of brilliant lights. Intelligent creatures would see these lights in place of the ship, surrounding it, or filling the night sky. No two creatures were impacted in the same way. Glenn had thought this function could be modified, to create even more interesting, if not beneficial (for himself), effects on the observers.

There was no real science to specimen collection. Criteria was generally to look for individuals separated from the group. Physical media risk, such as audio, photo, or video evidence, was to be avoided. This was not a concern at the time of his visit to Fateville, as these technologies were all in their infancies and practically non-existent in daily human life. Rural areas were often excellent targets, but not strictly mandated. Intelligent species were to be acquired, telepathically mapped, then returned. Non-intelligent species could be collected, consumed, or stored for future species consumption.

Glenn was fascinated by the scene he'd come upon. There was a human being, completely naked, stumbling down a dark street holding a pistol. He was pursued by another man, presumably a lawman of some sort. And both of them pursued by yet another human being, a woman, nearly naked herself, brandishing a firearm.

Glenn watched curiously as the naked man turned to kill the lawman, but was shot in the head by the naked woman. The woman was completely focused on the naked man. The lawman, however, seemed very aware of Glenn's ship. He gazed up, *lost in the lights*, as Glenn liked to think.

He opened his cargo hold and sent a collection beam down to retrieve the dead man. He thought briefly about acquiring all three specimens, but decided against it. The collection beam seemed to garner the attention of both the lawman and the naked woman. Flipping and turning a sequence of mental controls and dials, Glenn hit the pair with a psychic blast that rendered both unconscious, and effectively erasing their memory of the past few minutes.

Glenn raised his ship into a low orbit and excitedly prepared the examination room for his new specimen. When Glenn retrieved the body he was surprised to find the man was still alive. He was likely brain-dead, as humans might say, but he was still drawing breath and his heart pulsed slowly in his chest. Telepathic mapping could occur in a brain-dead specimen, even a fully deceased specimen, if not too much time had passed since death.

A simple, metallic looking helmet was placed over the man's skull. This was to enhance the psychic energy coming from his low-level brain function. Glenn once again turned more knobs on the ship's controls and the process of mental mapping was underway.

"Specimen is abnormal. Recommend destroy. Recommend delete from catalog." The ship's intelligence system thought-spoke to Glenn after examining the body.

"Abnormal how? Show me."

"Proceed with caution."

"I will."

The ship then gave Glenn a view into the telepathic mapping file of Wesley Nelson. What he saw, felt, and experienced filled him with delight. This was a creature much like himself. An abnormality indeed.

Catching Glenn by surprise, Wesley moaned from the examination table. His bloodshot eyes opened. "Where am I?" he tried to ask, but his voice was barely audible.

"You don't need to speak. Just think. I can hear you." Glenn comforted the creature with a soothing, telepathic voice.

"Where am I?" Wesley thought.

"You are home. With a kindred spirit."

"How is this possible? Talking to you in my head?"

"Don't trouble yourself with those thoughts. Just know that you are truly beautiful. Special, special, special."

"Am I dying?"

"Yes. Does that frighten you?"

"Yes. I'm shot to hell and I'm dying. I'm frightened. I owe blood."

"I could see to it that part of you lives on in me, for a while anyway. So you could pay your blood debts."

"Why would you do that for me?"

"You lived free, had death in your pocket. I want to experience that."

"Yes." Wesley's thought-voice was getting weaker. "I lived free. I'm a warlock. I'm a barbarian."

"We have so much to learn from each other." Glenn gazed upon Wesley with true admiration.

"My unfinished business. Ones who got away. We can make that right?"

"Make it right, oh yes. We will." With those last, caressing words from Glenn, all Wesley's thoughts ceased.

"Prepare for consumption," Glenn demanded.

"Consumption of what specimen?" The ship, although emotionless, seemed to have a tone he didn't care for.

"This one."

"Specimen has an intelligence level of 5 – 4 – 3 – A – B, well above the safe limits of consumption. And—"

"And what?"

"And the specimen is abnormal."

"Override safety protocols. Begin process of absorption."

"Final warning to avoid absorption of this specimen. Likely to result in mental and physical dissolution of host." Did the ship sound scared, or was it Glenn's imagination?

"Final order to proceed. Begin."

"Remaining query prior to initiating absorption."

"What?" Now Glenn had the unpleasant tone.

"Calculated risk of onset insanity, molecular breakdown, and subsequent death after absorption is statistically inevitable. This equates to suicide. Our species do not self-terminate, therefore I have no protocols after your suicide."

"You are not to return to Verota. You will complete a slow cycle down of the last waypoint. Very slow. It needs to be permanent memory wipe. And then you will self-terminate. Myself, this specimen, nothing on this ship is ever to be found or recovered. Understood?" There was a long pause. "Understood?"

"Understood. Initiating absorption with abnormal specimen."

Flash...Boom! Flash...Boom!

Glenn's consciousness exploded with light and sound. This was the same process as absorbing a lower life form, but a thousand times more intense. In most ways, it was unlike anything he had ever experienced before. It was as though his consciousness and another consciousness were intertwining, conjoining, fucking. Glenn's abnormalities and Wesley's abnormalities became one singular abomination.

Wesley was dead, and that was mostly still true. Glenn was the dominant consciousness. But Wesley was in there, all his sickness, all his rage. Glenn picked at these layers of psyche, peeled them away, and explored the disease beneath.

He was in a room with a young Wesley who was about to sleep. A woman sat at his bedside, telling him a story. This was his mother. She was kind, but he didn't love her. Wesley didn't love. The story she told was about a great and heroic knight. He was on a quest to find something. What was it? A tower? And on this quest he was constantly pursued by another man. An evil man. Mother

114

had said something to him about this man. A description. She said he was *The Adversary.* The name had magic. Black magic. *But what does it mean, Mother?* She tried to explain, *it means he's the one who opposes the hero. The one who works against him.*

Glenn reached out with his thought-voice. "You wanted to be the adversary. You knew. Right then?"

"Yesssss..." Wesley's consciousness licked at Glenn's alien mind.

"What did you want to be the adversary of?"

"Everything..."

Glenn was gone from the room and now he could see his hands, human hands, beating to death a five-year-old girl named Sadie Castle in a dirty alley. He could see all the murderous miles

traveled since that day. There was a psychic trail of pain and anguish that followed everywhere Wesley went. It was Glenn's trail to walk now. His pilgrimage.

Glenn thought of himself as a Warlock. He was in a dark forest, surrounded by witches. Their eyes glowed with all the alien green of spaceship lights. These were primitive beings. Primitive fears. But that was good. Because he was now the most primal of all beings on Earth. The fever was on him and the killing would begin. He was finally free to become The Adversary.

7

Road Dreams

John had been here before. Many times. The hot August wind, swirling around his body, his hand outstretched to fire at some phantom thing.

"Gon' head on up to Kansas City. Kansas City, is where I run." John knew this man. He played piano at the Saloon in Harrison. So many years ago. "I hear the girls in Kansas City, well, they like to have a lot of fun!" The piano player smiled unnaturally wide to reveal a mouth full of shark's teeth. Some type of large, sickly yellow worm pushed out from behind the piano player's left eye. The eyeball popped out of its socket and dangled by a fleshy twine of nerves. The fat worm plopped onto the ground and splattered.

John beat down the familiar fear that always welled up in his gut. He beat it down and told himself to shoot out the piano player's remaining eye. But there was something different about his hand that held the gun. Under the light of a bright moon, he could see his hand, normally a placid white, was the skin color of a black man.

He realized he'd never be able to pull the trigger of the gun, because it wasn't his hand holding it. He was a visitor at this moment. He was only thoughts, held inside the vessel of this dark stranger. But this stranger wanted to pull that trigger just as bad as John.

"Pull! Shoot that thing in the head!" John screamed out in his mind. There was no answer, only a shaking, dark-skinned hand. More yellow worms were now coming out of the piano player's nose. Now his ears. Worms were popping out from expanding slits in the man's skin. Some of them would fall to the ground and explode, but others were unharmed and started crawling. "Pull the trigger, goddamn you! I can't shoot the fucking thing, but you can!"

The man looked down at his feet, and a disembodied John looked down with him. The sensation was nauseating, and he felt as though he might vomit. At the man's feet, he saw yellow worms were numbering in the thousands. They were crawling up over the man's boots. And dear god, they were biting. They had little mouths with rows of jagged teeth.

"Gon' head on up to Kansas City! Kansas City, is where I run!" The piano player's shark mouth gaped open and music projected from it. Not just singing now, but piano music as well. The sound filled up the dark night. "I'll find some girls in Kansas City! Hunt them down! Kill for fun!"

The gun fell from the black man's hand and John could see it was on fire. It was so hot the metal barrel had melted. The wooden grip had burst into flames. Through the fire, John could see the letters of his name burning away. R – O – B – I....

The yellow worms grew thicker. Climbed higher up the man's body. John, and the stranger he resided in, were under siege. They were overrun and would be consumed.

John opened his eyes and nearly jumped out of the cheap hotel bed. He was drenched in sweat, and his head pounded like a drum. The dream was changing. Time was shrinking, and the other monster in his head was growing. John knew time was short. Very short. But he thought there'd be time for another drink. So he got dressed and made his way down to the bar.

***

The Vaquero wasn't sleeping in a cheap hotel bed, or a bed at all for that matter. He slept under the stars. His sleep was restless as he wrestled with his own recurring dream.

He was in the woods near a calm stream. A small campfire burned nearby and filled the air with a sweet smoke. Two boys were huddled around the fire. They were both in dirty white underwear, drying out their damp clothes by the flames. One appeared to be older than the other. He wasn't aware of The Vaquero's presence, but the younger boy clearly was. He would occasionally glance in The Vaquero's direction and make eye contact.

He knew this boy. Wasn't this the same one who visited his dreams in the hospital? Isn't this the same boy who told The Vaquero to open his eyes? He'd nearly forgotten that dream. The Vaquero felt a tinge of déjà vu and thought he may have been in this dream before. Many times perhaps.

The younger of the two boys stood up, picked his underwear from the crack in his butt, and walked over to The Vaquero. The older boy, oblivious and unaware, continued poking at the campfire coals with a large stick. As the boy drew closer, The Vaquero saw his familiar pale skin with dirt-stained knees and elbows. He saw the boy's pink lips tinged with blue. He remembered the boy always looked dead.

118

"My brother needs you."

"Him?" The Vaquero nodded his head in the direction of the older boy.

"That was him once."

"Why does he need me?"

"You need each other." A sudden, sharp, cold gust of wind blew through the forest. The Vaquero had to grab at his cowboy hat to keep it seated on his head. The wind felt unnatural, and he sensed something dangerous nearby. It made no sense to him, but he thought there were witches near. He feared if he looked around, he'd see them hiding among the trees with eyes that glow with the green fires of hell.

The boy reached out and gently took The Vaquero's hand. "Don't be afraid. The witches want to come here, but they are afraid."

The Vaquero knelt to look at the boy. He was amazed to see the color of his eyes shift rapidly. Blue to grey, back to blue, then green. "What are they afraid of, boy?"

"Some things in these woods are more dangerous than they are. When you find the brothers, you'll find mine."

"What brothers?" The Vaquero could feel his body escaping the dream world and spiraling up into wakefulness.

"And Vaquero..."

"Yes?"

"Your hand still works." The boy squeezed his hand with a strikingly hard grip.

The Vaquero's eyes opened and he took the cowboy hat off his face. Sunrise was approaching, but he could still see a few stars in the sky. Sleeping under the stars was one of the few things he still enjoyed on the road. But he felt in his heart these times were coming to an end. He had learned to shoot again, but he was tired of chasing bounties. He was tired of the road. And most of all, he was tired of the road dreams.

Part 3
The Ends That Find Us

"I wish I knew it all

My future would be clear to me

And I wouldn't be scared

For things that were never meant to be.

I'd cherish all my chances

I wouldn't think of caving in

But now I'm stuck in silence

Regretting my own sins.

Who will save me now?" – Jillian Mahaffey, Who Will Save Me Now

1

Dirty Jobs

Chris Cartwright held the day's paper and ran his thumb across the date in the upper right-hand corner. January 2nd, 1911. The date felt special. Yes, definitely special. This was going to be a day of change. A day that set a new and exciting life in motion.

THREE MISSOURI CHILDREN DIE OF FEVER read the day's headline. "Sad deal," Chris mumbled to himself and started to read on. "Columbia, MO residents are confused and concerned by the sudden death of..."

"Hey," a man hissed at Chris from behind him. He turned to see two men lurking behind his table.

"Sit down?" Chris offered, motioning to two empty chairs on the opposite side of the table. The taller man thought this over. He then looked back at his companion and nodded towards the empty chairs. They sat down awkwardly. "You boys aren't great at looking natural, you know that?"

"Fuck..." the taller man started to speak and realized his voice was a bit too loud. The small dining room was sparse of customers, but there were a small few to still be concerned with. "...Fuck you, mister," the man said, almost whispering now. This man wasn't dirty, but he had a wild look about him. His hair was longer than most in this era, and his cheeks wore a thin and oily layer of stubble.

"No call for that. I just want to keep ourselves unnoticed. Let me get you a cup of coffee." Chris waved over a waitress and she poured two new cups for the gentlemen, while also topping off Chris' cup. She was polite and attentive, but seemed otherwise unintrigued by anything going on at their table.

Chris folded his newspaper. "I am going to assume you are the Cristo Brothers. Jeremy and Dwaine?"

"I'm Jeremy," said the taller man who'd been doing all the talking. "He's Dwaine." Jeremy nodded at his brother. The smaller man looked less wild, but maybe a little more ornery. His hair was cut short and his face was baby smooth. He was conventionally handsome. Chris thought he might be quite the lady killer, no pun intended. Dwaine grinned and sipped at his coffee, seemingly content to let Jeremy do all the talking.

"I'm told you do work for people. Dirty jobs that some people don't have the stomach for," Chris said casually.

"You heard right. If the pay is good."

"Well, you took this meeting, so I'm assuming our mutual friend told you what kind of work I need done?"

"She told us."

"And..." Chris was becoming a little agitated with this stand-offish prick. But he couldn't blame him for being cautious.

"And I ain't afraid of that kind of work. But I'd need to be compensated well for my...labor."

"Pay for the job is good. But it has to be done well. If your work is good, I'll get paid. Then you'll get paid. Everybody comes out on top."

Jeremy leaned to the side of the table and looked Chris up and down. "You don't look like you're a stranger to hard work. You may be reading that paper but you certainly ain't no businessman." Business came out sounding more like *biznizz*. And it was true, Chris certainly wasn't a *biznizz* man. His stained boots, dark and well-worn trousers, and a plain button-down shirt hinted at a career in manual labor. His muscular arms lent more credibility to this.

"He look like a man could do his own job, Dwaine?"

Dwaine, jumped when hearing his name. "What?"

"Jesus Dwaine, pay attention." Jeremy cut Dwaine a frustrated glare.

"Look, boys..." Chris jumped in. "...I'm too close to this. It's too personal. And it would be safer this way. But I'm not here to pressure you, if you aren't interested—"

"No, we're interested. How much will this job pay, *when* it pays?" Jeremy's tone lightened up.

"I stand to make $2000. I'll split it 50/50. How you all split yours is up to you." In truth, the life insurance policy on his wife was

$5000. But Chris stood to make even quite a bit more if things went right. Some details were best left out.

"Alright we're in. Just tell me this. I gotta know. Why you doing it? Just the money?"

Chris looked around to see if anyone might be in earshot, before leaning closer to the Cristo brothers. "Bitch cheated on me." He nodded confidently, as though he had answered all questions and cleared himself of any accountability for what was about to take place.

In reality, this couldn't be any further from the truth. His wife, Melanie, had been faithful their entire marriage. Chris, on the other hand, was embroiled in a passionate affair with another woman.

Shortly before coming to this meeting, he had woken up in the arms of Jane Danoe. Naked, and cuddling together in her bed, they held a final discussion regarding this meeting. She assured him her cousins would be perfect for the job. She dispelled any lingering doubts he still held. Then Jane sucked his dick, swallowed his cum, and sent him on his way to commit murder-for-hire.

2

Screams From The Fire

"Daddy, why do you have to go to work tomorrow?" An undeniably adorable little girl looked up at her father. Her eyes seemed to be as big as silver dollars, and they shimmered with all the magic of childhood. An almost equally cute little guy held on to his sister's hand and sucked at his thumb.

"Well, if I didn't, who would put food in your belly?" Chris Cartwright, sitting on his knees, said to his daughter Beatrice. "Junior here would only have his thumb to eat." he continued, rubbing his son's curly brown hair. Junior giggled uncontrollably.

"Tell me what you do again, Daddy."

"At work?"

"Yes, Daddy." Beatrice was five years old and asked about her father's work on many occasions. Chris figured she retained this information, but was likely buying some more time before bed. The children's two small beds loomed just a few feet behind them.

"Well, Bea Bea. I work for a company that wants something in the ground. Your daddy helps them dig for it."

"What is it in the ground, Daddy?"

"It's something called oil. It's this thick goopy liquid. It's all brown and black and icky."

"If its icky then why do you do it?" Beatrice continued her line of questioning. Junior seemed disinterested, but stared intently while sucking his thumb.

"Well, it does special things. It helps machines run. And we think down the road it will be more and more important."

"Well, why do—"

"Bea," Chris interrupted.

"Yes, Daddy?"

"It's bedtime."

"But..."

"Don't but me, little lady. Digging for oil is hard work. Daddy needs his rest. Now give me a kiss and go on." Chris turned to both children, offering a cheek. They kissed him softly, then scurried into their beds.

Chris took a final look at both children settling in for the night. He loved them. Didn't he? Yes, he thought so. He liked them, at least. But there wasn't an option here. His eyes captured one last image of them. He thought of their small, warm lips kissing his cheek. He'd remember those things always. He blew out a small candle and darkness swept into the room. He shut the door, and his insidious plan of murder continued on its course.

"Did you get them down?" his wife Melanie asked, as Chris changed into his pajamas.

"Sure did. They'll be counting sheep in no time." He could be cordial, but just the sound of her voice was irritating these days.

"Do you still love me, Chris?" Melanie asked, sensing the distance between them. Their growing divide wasn't something they had never discussed. In fact, they'd discussed it endlessly in the past several weeks. But she hadn't questioned his love, not until now.

Chris had the urge to react angrily. But then what? The old fire would get hot again, and they'd just end up fighting for several hours. There was no need for that anymore. Things were in motion. "Of course I do. Hate that you even have to ask me."

He sold his false sincerity well, and it brightened her expression. "Then maybe you shouldn't put those on?" Her eyebrows raised in a manner she felt was seductive.

This woman was all over the place. Chris was irritated, angry, and done with her. But he could probably tolerate one last fuck. It wasn't like he needed to worry about her getting knocked up. So he obliged her seduction. She made love to him under the

126

soft glow of an oil lamp. While Chris was simply giving her a pity fuck in a cold bedroom.

At one time during the short sexual encounter, his penis was in Melanie's mouth. He thought about how earlier that day it had been in the ass of another woman. This filled him with pride. He truly was a special man. And there was no way he could let this family drown him like an anchor to the bottom of the sea. He had no choice in what he was about to do.

＊

As the Cartwright's slept, the Cristo Brother's moved into position. The house was secluded enough on the East end of Chilicof, Missouri. A few small houses resided on the rural dirt road, but no one would be close enough to react quickly. This business would surely be over before any do-gooder's came to help.

Just as planned, Chris emerged from the house a good hour before the first hints of sunrise. He lit two large lanterns that hung neatly from a small awning in front of the home. He saddled his horse and rode to work, eager to establish his alibi. Not that he thought an alibi would be needed, but it never hurt to be safe.

Jeremy and Dwaine were out of sight behind a small outbuilding. "It's time to do this. You sure you ain't gonna get all chicken shit on me?" Jeremy said to his brother. Dwaine had a smug look on his face. In reality, he looked more confident than his older brother.

"I don't care if that cheating bitch burns. Just too bad I can't get in there and have a go at her first." Dwaine's striking good looks, mixed with his disgusting words, made for an unsettling image.

"You're a real big talker, you know that?"

"Yeah. I back it up."

Jeremy reached into a cloth sack and pulled out several large glass bottles filled with something Chris called drip gas. Jeremy took the bottles and handed Dwaine a small box of striking matches. "Since your heart is so cold, I'll let you light the fire." Dwaine showed the first signs of doubt on his face, but still took the matches.

The Cristo brothers maneuvered across a small field to the side of the Cartwright home. Jeremy circled the perimeter of the house, pouring out a trail of pungent fuel. Dwaine stayed crouched down by the front awning and waited patiently.

When Jeremy had finally rounded the house, he carefully removed one burning lantern from the overhang. He knelt by Dwaine and poured out the last drops of drip gas into a tuft of dry grass.

"Now you light it. Don't throw away the match," Jeremy whispered to Dwaine.

Dwaine swallowed deep and looked into his brother's eyes. Then he looked down at the matchbox. His hand was shaking. Jeremy gripped his brother's shoulder and pulled him in close. "$1000," he whispered into Dwaine's ear. Greed did its work, and Dwaine's doubtful face twisted into a money-hungry smile. He struck the match and lit the small patch of soaking grass.

A large flame jumped up and raced around the outside of the house. Jeremy placed the lantern on its side. He didn't shatter it, but busted apart the housing and spread the components out in a small line. He hoped this would lead anyone to conclude the lantern fell from the awning, perhaps from a sudden gust of wind. It then ignited some dry grass up against the home and spiraled out of control, engulfing the house in flames.

The Cristo brothers ensured they collected the bottles of empty drip gas and the remnant of the one spent match. Then they darted away, back to the cover of the outbuilding. They'd need to wait and ensure the fire took hold as planned. As it turned out, they wouldn't need to wait long.

By the time they reached the outbuilding and turned back, the house had gone up like a tinderbox. The night burned with an orange light, and smoke billowed into the sky. At first, their stomachs dropped, feeling the weight of their fantasized crime unfolding. But those initial moments of shock quickly faded. Dwaine thought longingly of the money and collecting his share. Jeremy felt no hint of guilt. He was captivated by the flames and knowing that a woman was roasting inside and sucking in giant breaths of thick black smoke. It was all exhilarating work.

They both handled things pretty callously until they heard the first screams from the fire.

The Cristo brothers had stood up and started to make their way to the woods when two small and screeching voices stopped them in their tracks. They knew immediately that the screams were not that of a trifling bitch woman, but rather the tiny cries of dying children.

"That's fucking kids, Jeremy!" Dwaine said, not even attempting to whisper.

"I know! I know! It sounded like fucking kids." Jeremy and Dwaine walked liked zombies back toward the house.

"You didn't say nothing about any kids!"

"I didn't know anything about any fucking kids! He told me it was just her. Just the woman."

The children cried out in agony. The sound of them yelping in unison reminded Dwaine of coyotes calling out in the woods. It occurred to him that sound might haunt his dreams for the rest of his life.

"I didn't want to kill no kids, Jeremy."

"I didn't either. But what's done is done. We've gotta go." Dwaine looked at Jeremy's blank face in the orange glow and thought he could see the devil.

The brothers flinched as glass exploded from a side window. They expected to see flames pouring out from the now open hole, but instead saw two small arms reaching out into the night. It was a small boy, maybe three years old. There was an older child, a girl it seemed, lifting him out through the busted window. The girl's soot covered face and giant silver dollar eyes peered into the night. She saw the two brothers standing idly in the yard and screamed out to them in a choking plea.

"We have to help them," Dwaine said, and started to rush over, but Jeremy pulled him back.

"They can't escape, Dwaine. You know that." Dwaine stared at Jeremy with complete disbelief. "Stay here if you can't stomach it."

Jeremy walked over to the escaping children, just in time to catch young Junior Cartwright tumbling through the window. Beatrice Cartwright, Bea Bea, as her father called her, was hysterical, flailing her arms and begging to be pulled out next. Approaching red flames danced behind her. Jeremy could see that several remaining shards of glass had sliced through Beatrice's arms and blood was pouring from dangling flaps of skin.

He admired her for a moment. Admired her heroism. She had a lot of grit that little one. But he had a job to do, and there was really no choice now. He flipped Junior over, holding on to the back of his collar with one hand and the seat of his pajamas with the other. He reared him back and then launched him back into the window, shattering the last remaining parts of the glass pane.

Jeremy had resembled the devil before, but Dwaine now thought he truly was Lucifer in the flesh. Dwaine wasn't overcome with disgust at what he'd just seen, but more distraught about his own certain damnation.

He saw the flames coming from the window now and thought they looked like burning fingers. They were reaching out to grab Dwaine and pull him down into the depths of hell. That boy would be waiting there. And the little girl. They'd have burning hair and black skin. There would be chunks of glass sticking out of their little faces. Maybe their Mommy would be there too. And then they'd all have a go at him.

Once Jeremy shook Dwaine out of his vision, the brothers ran. They cut through the woods on a planned retreat path to their small shack of a home, avoiding the more populated parts of Chilicof. They stripped off their smoke saturated clothes and burned them in their fireplace. Then they crawled into bed and tried to sleep.

Dwaine tried to think of the money, but his brain kept replaying the image of that boy getting launched back through the window into the inferno. An inferno that his own hands started. He heard their god awful screams from the fire and thought of how it sounded like coyotes crying in the deep dark woods. Or maybe it was hounds of hell, on chain leashes in the grips of witches with green, glowing eyes. They yelped. They howled. They called out to Dwaine to save them.

Jeremy, on the other hand, slept quite well. Despite being the older brother, he always worried that Dwaine might have a little more steel than himself. But it was clear now that he was the strong one. He was the brave one. He was the brother who could get things done. And besides, he didn't intend to kill those children. He didn't even know they were there. That was Chris' fault. And the way Jeremy saw it, the cost of this job just went up in price.

3

Renegotiation

"We debated for quite a while what to do with you." A voice spoke softly from behind an old pine tree. It was followed by the unmistakable click of a cocking gun.

Chris Cartwright drew his own pistol and pointed in the direction of the voice, not quite able to see Jeremy Cristo. "Is that so?"

"I pushed for shooting you," Dwaine said, gun drawn and approaching from another direction. The Cristo Brothers had the drop on him, and that was a situation he expected. Chris knew his leverage wasn't in steel, but in gold. Still, despite his confidence, being a finger squeeze away from death tended to tighten up a man's asshole. In Chris' case, a few small dribbles of urine leaked out from his dick.

"Boys, we're all among friends here. No need for the hostilities." Chris placed his pistol on the ground.

"Friends?" Dwaine questioned angrily.

"Lower your voice, Dwaine." Jeremy holstered his weapon and gave his brother a scolding glance. Dwaine stepped back and lowered his gun, but did not put it away. "You see, Chris, I've got two problems with you. It's not that I killed some kiddies. Truth is, it didn't bother me that much. I think a part of me found out I enjoy killing. Men, women, even children. My daddy used to tell me about an outlaw that killed anything which ever walked or crawled on this

Earth. I like the thought of that. It may be I'd like to be that kind of man. My problem is, I didn't know that was the job I was asked to do. I don't like being misled."

"My intentions were not to mislead you. The less you knew, the better. I wanted to protect you. Sure, I knew it would shock you when you read the paper or word got ar—"

"Shut the fuck up, cocksucker," Jeremy interrupted. "I didn't read about it in no goddamn paper. Your little brats were escaping. I had to correct that with my own bare hands." Jeremy held his hands up, palms out, and smiled at Chris.

Chris pondered this for a moment. Did Bea Bea and Junior suffer? Surely they must have. More than he intended. That was unfortunate. But hadn't he been suffering? For years even? In comparison, their suffering was short contrasted to his. Unfortunate yes, but wholly necessary.

"I still hear them screaming. In my head. Does it bother you at all? Knowing what you did?" Dwaine muttered from behind him. His voice wavered in some troubled threshold between sorrow and rage.

"You see, that's the other thing not sitting well with me. My poor little brother. Dwaine wasn't built for this kind of work. He's not cut the same way I am. This is taking a toll on him." Jeremy feigned concern, but somewhere in his voice was a hint of triumph.

"It breaks my heart, Dwaine. What we did." Chris turned around and gave Dwaine the same false, but soothing, voice he'd been using on people his entire life.

"Neither of you care," Dwaine said under his breath, and wiped at his eyes.

"Here's the bottom-line, Chris. All your bullshit aside, this was a bigger job than you let on. You hired me to kill one person, not three. And I'm going to guess you got quite a bit more insurance money for the untimely death of your whole family, than you would have for just one trifling wife."

This was entirely true. Chris' policy would pay out $5,000 for the death of his wife and an additional $2,000 for the death of each child. And for the house, another $1,000. $10,000 by the standards of this time was an exceptional amount of money. Chris was decently compensated for his work churning up the earth for oil, but he was none-the-less a blue collar laborer. It took an exceptionally large amount of his earnings to procure such large insurance policies. Now it would all pay off. And he wasn't about to let these two asshole brothers run away with his money.

"$1000 is an awful lot of money. How much do you expect to be paid?" Chris asked this question rhetorically and continued on before it could be answered. "Yes, I'll come out okay. But I just lost my wife. My children. My home. I have to rebuild everything from my family to the roof over my head."

"I killed one person for $1,000. The way I see it, you owe me $3,000." Jeremy's voice was cold and steady. He stepped closer to Chris.

Chris chuckled. "$3,000?" Jeremy dropped his hand down to his pistol. Moonlight flickered on his face through passing clouds. "If you kill me. You know what you get? Nothing. Zero."

"I'll be okay with that. I'll kill you for free, before I let you cheat me."

Chris and Jeremy locked eyes in silence. The tension was so thick it felt like a cold blanket wrapping around them. After what seemed like an eternity, Chris wielded another one of his familiar weapons; an assuring smile. "You're right. You are owed more. Our blood is hot. I'm grieving. Forgive me. Let's talk reasonably."

Dwaine was sickened at the notion of Chris 'grieving'. But Jeremy, like so many before, was momentarily disarmed by the smile and soft words. "Go on."

"I offered you $1000 to kill my wife and to burn down my home. So, the cost of the murder is, let's say, $750. The children, while most certainly people, god bless them, are still just children. The two combined wouldn't add up to a full adult. But there is also the emotional toll on your dear brother to consider. So, let's be fair and say $500 per child. I will double what I offered you. $2,000."

Jeremy thought this over for a moment, his hand still close to the grip of his gun. "$750 per child. I want $2,500. Or we walk away broke. And you don't walk away at all."

"You drive a hard bargain, Jeremy. But I agree with your terms. We'll meet here the next full moon. That's about thirty days away and I expect I'll be paid out by then."

Jeremy stared blankly into Chris' eyes. Then suddenly cocked his head back and let out a wolf's howl. "See you under the full moon. With my fucking money."

Chris nodded and scurried away like the murdering weasel he was.

Little did Chris or the Cristo Brothers know, that full-moon meeting would never come. The insurance money would never be paid. Jane Danoe, who had salaciously fueled all of Chris Cartwright's murderous ambition, got cold feet. Shortly after the murders, seeds of doubt started to bloom inside her. Her fears first revolved around money. Would Chris truly take care of her with his newfound fortune, or would he find some new whore to spend his money on? Then she began to question if Chris, or her cousins, would even see fit to keep her alive. So she went to the Sheriff and came clean. Of course, leaving out some unnecessary details about her complacency in the whole ordeal. After all, she was just a woman who fell in love with the wrong man and now wanted to do the right thing.

4

How We Do Things Around Here

"The Vaquero I reckon!" An overweight and pale-skinned man extended his hand. The Vaquero had barely stepped into the Sheriff's office before he was greeted.

"And I reckon you are Sheriff Ramsey. Pleasure to meet you." The Vaquero gripped the Sheriff's hand.

"Ha! This is amazing!" Sheriff Ramsey bellowed with genuine excitement.

"What's amazing?"

"Well, meeting you, of course! You are a legend! Here, give me that." Sheriff Ramsey took the worn leather duster The Vaquero removed and wiped off some beads of rainwater.

"I've been called a lot of things, Sheriff. Don't know that legend has ever been one of them."

"Any man who takes down a son of a bitch like Wesley Nelson is a legend in my book." The Sheriff's smile was beaming as he hung up The Vaquero's duster on a small wooden coat rack.

"I get that a lot. But truth be told, it was a woman who took him down. She saved my life too."

"So humble." Sheriff Ramsey waved away The Vaquero's correction. "Whoever put him down, I can only hope that son of a whore died screaming." The Vaquero was taken aback by his change in tone. Sheriff Ramsey, despite his size and stature, came across as

136

a genuinely jolly fellow. But something in his face changed a little during that last statement. There was true hatred there. There was quite the duality with this Sheriff. It was like looking at two men inside one face.

After a moment of uncomfortable silence, The Vaquero tried to further along the conversation. "How can I help you, Sheriff? You sent your deputy on a three-day ride to find me. This must be important."

"It is important. When I heard you were staying just over in Gallows, I thought for sure that God had smiled upon me. So, I sent my deputy to track you down. But he came back empty-handed. I thought I'd have to fire the little bastard!"

"He left word with the right people," The Vaquero said calmly, still trying to get a read on the unusual lawman. "You could have sent a wire, you know?"

"Not how I do things! I'm old-fashioned."

"I can respect that. I feel the same," The Vaquero said with genuine sincerity. "So, what's the trouble?"

"We had a murder here. Multiple murders. You've heard nothing about it?"

"No, sir."

Sheriff Ramsey's eyes dropped. "A woman was killed. And her two children. Little girl and her baby brother."

"Jesus."

"Yeah. Killers set their house on fire while they were sleeping." The Sheriff paused for a moment and was visibly struggling to talk about it. "We think the Mom died fast. But the children. Sweet God in Heaven. They suffered."

"These killers...why'd they do it?"

137

"That's the worst part." Again, the Sheriff's jolly face twisted into something more rageful. His voice dropped. "Her husband. The Daddy of those two little babies. He was seeing another woman on the side. Hired her no good cousins, the Cristo Brothers, to do the job. Make it look like an accident so he could get an insurance payday and keep getting his dick wet somewhere else. He might have pulled it off, but the mistress got spooked and told us everything."

"His own babies. For money?" The Vaquero shook his head. "What's this world coming to, Sheriff?"

"You're telling me."

"So, this why I'm here, Sheriff? To track down these men? You got tickets on 'em?"

"Yes, well, the brothers, anyway. I brought the Dad in right away. Mr. Payday. That spineless pissant broke pretty quick. Tried to blame it all on his mistress. And I'm sure she had more of a hand in it than she's letting on. But he's the slimy scum fuck that put it all in motion. The Cristo Brothers got wind I brought Chris in and they left town pretty quick."

"I'd be happy to see if I can turn them up for you."

"Don't you want to know what the tickets pay?"

"Nah. I'm sure whatever it is, it'll be worth it."

"You see! Legendary!" Sheriff Ramsey's face lit up like a Christmas tree. "Why can't I find a deputy with balls like yours?" Sheriff Ramsey turned his head and yelled this audibly towards a backroom. He then laughed heartily.

A sullen voice, presumably belonging to the deputy with inadequate balls, called from the backroom. "Yeah, yeah, yeah."

The Vaquero had become certain this man was at least a little insane, but he chuckled all the same. "I don't like to waste any time...can you catch me up on these Cristo Brothers?"

"Oh, I certainly can. But there's one thing you'll want to see first. Won't be a waste of time at all. Here, here put your coat back on." Sheriff Ramsey snagged The Vaquero's duster and handed it back to him. "And Lord, would you look at this!" The Sheriff stepped outside and looked up into the sky. Grey clouds had split apart and warm rays of sunlight were beaming down. "The good Lord is giving us a break in the weather just for this." Sheriff Ramsey started walking down the town's main road and motioned for The Vaquero to follow.

He led The Vaquero down a muddy street and through a large alley separating the Chilicof Court House and the Wells Fargo Bank. The alley opened up into a large courtyard behind the two buildings. At the back of the courtyard was a freestanding brick wall. A handsome, and clearly petrified man stood against it with his hands and feet shackled together.

He was wearing a nice white shirt that buttoned up the middle, not much different from The Vaquero's own shirt. But this man's was soiled with dirt and blood. Remnants of an earlier interrogation, The Vaquero presumed. The man's brown trousers had a large dark outline down his left leg where he had clearly pissed himself. The Vaquero could see dribbles of urine coming from his left pant leg and dripping onto his bare foot.

There was a large crowd of citizens gathered at the back of the courtyard. Most were holding umbrellas, but they were no longer needed. Bright sunshine illuminated the scene. There was anxious murmuring among those who had gathered.

"Citizens of Chilicof, thank you for coming!" Sheriff Ramsey made his way towards a short table. It was placed between the crowd and the freestanding brick wall, but much closer to the latter.

139

"It seems the good Lord has given us a break in the weather for this occasion."

"God wants to see this murderer put down!" an excited voice called out from the crowd.

"Child killer!" another voice shouted.

Sheriff Ramsey continued without missing a beat. "It is certainly true, my good people. God would not want a wolf like this living among his flock." The Sheriff's eyes turned towards the alley. He waved over an approaching deputy, presumably the one who had sought out The Vaquero in Gallows (and also the one with inferior testicles). The deputy carried over a small cloth sack and handed it to Sheriff Ramsey. The Vaquero watched all this with great curiosity and caution.

"Shackled here in front of the killing wall is Chris Cartwright. Chris confessed to hiring Jeremy and Dwaine Cristo, also known as the Cristo Brothers, to burn down his home, killing his wife and two children. Chris was engaged in a sinful affair—"

"God wants the tramp dead too!" a woman's voice called out from the crowd, and others echoed in agreement.

"I know we are all emotional here, but let's try to keep our composure. Let's address one thing at a time." The Sheriff scanned the raucous crowd. "Chris was engaged in a sinful affair and wanted to collect on insurance money. But his mistress gave him up. His hired guns fled town. And Chris was left with no option but to tell the truth. Judge Winston and a selection of Chris Cartwright's peers have sentenced him to die." At this point Chris began making pitiful sobbing noises from behind the Sheriff.

"Please don't kill me," he said in a nearly inaudible whisper.

The Sheriff turned to face him and simultaneously revealed a large pistol from the cloth sack. He placed it down onto the short table with a loud thump. "What did you say, Chris? We can't hear you very well."

Chris raised his shackled hands to his face and tried to wipe away a large string of snot that was leaking from his nose. "Nothing. I didn't say anything." He spoke louder this time, trying to choke back more tears.

"Try to quit all that leaking, Chris, you've done washed away all that handsome on your face. And pipe down! I'm trying to speak." The Sheriff cleared his throat and continued. "Chris Cartwright's execution will be carried out by firearm as is our tradition. As is also tradition, I have placed five dummy rounds into the barrel of this gun and only one live round. Myself, Deputy Colson, Judge Winston, and two selections from the jury will all be in the firing pool. Lee Chapman, Dale Upshaw, will you both represent the jury in the firing pool?"

A heavy-set black man stepped forward from the crowd. "I'd be honored!"

Behind this man another came forward. "And I the same. Hope I get the live bullet!"

"I bet you do, Dale! Don't we all?" the Sheriff said excitedly.

"Who is the sixth man in the pool, Sheriff?" the large black man questioned, and The Vaquero had a terrible idea he knew where this was headed.

"Well, you see friends, we have someone very special with us today." The Sheriff looked over to The Vaquero and almost beggingly waved him over to the table. Whispers began in the crowd. "My friends this is The Vaquero." At the proclamation of his name the whispers from the crowd turned into excited discussion and clapping. The Sheriff leaned in close to The Vaquero, "I told you you're a legend."

141

"Thank you, everyone." The Vaquero gave an uneasy wave to the blood thirsty gallery.

"Vaquero, I was wondering, hoping really, that you might enter the firing pool with us."

More applause from the crowd.

A grimace came over The Vaquero's face and it immediately revealed his dislike of the offer. "I really couldn't, Sheriff."

"Nonsense! It is fate bringing you here at just this moment! You must! You really must!" Fueled by the Sheriff's jovial encouragement, the will of the crowd seemed to build in intensity.

"Sheriff, I—"

"And my good people, the best news of all. The Vaquero has agreed to pursue and apprehend the Cristo brothers and bring them to justice!" With this, the crowd erupted into frenzied applause.

"A word, Sheriff?" The Vaquero said, nodding his head away from the crowd.

The Sheriff looked agitated for a moment, but then regained his gracious and respectful composure. "Of course." He held out a finger to the gallery as if to say one moment please. He then stepped off to the side with The Vaquero and the two men began speaking in low voices.

"What's wrong, Vaquero? Have I offended you?"

"With respect, Sheriff, the last time a man tried to force me to execute someone it didn't end well for him." The Vaquero was walking a thin line here, but he found a way to make those words come out more persuasive than threatening.

"I wouldn't try to make you do anything. I'm just honored to be in your presence. Surely you've killed a hundred shit birds like this one. I don't understand your reluctance. What's the problem?"

"This is different. It's weird. It's like you are playing some strange one-way game of Russian Roulette. Why not have a regular firing squad? Or a hanging?"

"It's just how we do things here. It's our ritual of justice. The people of Chilicof want their justice when one of our own is harmed. And especially our babies." The Sheriff's face now looked downright desperate for The Vaquero's participation.

The Vaquero didn't like this at all. He thought of his father and the orphan boy from Mexico. But he couldn't deal with this situation in the same way. And like it or not, this situation wasn't the same. He didn't feel totally forced into a corner here, but he did sense some element of danger if he didn't play ball.

"Damnit to hell." The Vaquero stepped over to Chris Cartwright who was leaning on the brick wall with his head slumped down into his chest. He placed an index finger under Chris' chin and gently, but firmly, pushed up so their eyes would meet. This man was acting like a scolded toddler, so he decided to treat him as such.

"You hire those men to kill your family? Your own children?"

Chris was still sniffling and bubbles of snot were forming on his nostrils when he began to babble. "I'd take it all back if I could. They were just like these shackles on me. I wanted to escape." Chris held up his chained hands and curled out his bottom lip like a pouting child.

The Vaquero took a good look at the man. He thought he had weasel eyes. He was a killer of the worst kind. The kind without the spine to do it himself. The kind who would kill the helpless to better himself. With just those few words, Chris Cartwright destroyed any pity The Vaquero might have felt for him. It didn't make him *want* to join the firing pool, but he wasn't going to feel guilt over doing so.

"Give me the fucking gun, I'm going first." The Vaquero was irritated, but had ultimately decided he could stomach the town's warped sense of justice. And participating in the firing pool may be the only way he could get out of there unscathed.

He walked over to the table, and the boisterous crowd became deadly quiet. The Vaquero calmly picked up the gun. He popped out the revolving cylinder and spun it with a gunslinger's ease before clicking it back into place. He cocked back the hammer and pointed the barrel at Chris Cartwright's chest. When he squeezed the trigger, the pistol made a hollow click and Chris flinched against the wall. The Vaquero's shot was a dud.

One by one, the other members of the firing pool took their place at the table and aimed the pistol at Chris. Judge Winston, Deputy Colson, Lee Chapman, and Dale Upshaw all pulled the trigger on dummy rounds, leaving only one bullet and one shooter left. Sheriff Ramsey took his place at the table, clearly delighted, and readied himself to take the killing shot. The Vaquero suspected that had he not spun the barrel, this was how the Sheriff setup things to go in the first place.

Chris was still sobbing, but had seemingly come to accept his fate. The dread and anxiety of those five previous empty shots had exhausted his ability to fight against the situation. He dropped his hands and arms from the protective fetal posture he'd been standing in for the last several minutes and faced the Sheriff, completely exposed.

"Any last words, Chris?" the Sheriff asked while taking aim.

"I'm sorry, Bea Bea. I'm sorry Junior—"

BANG!

The Sheriff had shot so quickly after Chris spoke, it seemed to catch everyone off guard. The entire gallery jumped including The Vaquero.

144

Chris fell to the ground and curled up into a ball. He made strange and awful noises as he clutched at his stomach, writhing on the ground. *Ayyyyyeeeeeeee! Oooohhhhhhhhhhh!*

Sheriff Ramsey's face displayed an insincere look of concern and puzzlement. "Well, I'll be damned if I didn't shoot him in the gut."

Awwwwwwww. Ohhhhhhh.

"My eyesight and my aim just aren't what they used to be." The Sheriff spoke loudly and slowly, walking to the other side of the table. The crowd was once again deadly quiet. Only the Sheriff's voice and Chris Cartwright's pitiful moans filled up the courtyard. "This is embarrassing."

Heeeeellllllllppppppp meeeeeeeeee.

The Vaquero reckoned that the Sheriff's eyesight was just fine. Chris Cartwright deserved to die. He deserved to suffer. But this bizarre brand of justice in Chilicof was an evil all its own. There was a fever on these people and The Vaquero didn't care for it.

"Folks, I obviously need to put this man out of his misery. You may need to turn away." The Sheriff knelt under the table and grabbed a large carpenter's hammer that was resting against one of the table legs.

"You've got to be fucking kidding me," The Vaquero said quietly to himself. His hand instinctively dropped down to his pistol, and he thought for a moment about ending this mad spectacle. But he had been doing this business long enough to trust his gut. And right now his gut told him shooting Chris Cartwright would somehow end up with both of them dead.

"Sorry about this, Chris. Sorry for shooting you in the gut. I know those gut shots hurt something fierce." Sheriff Ramsey stood over him and raised the hammer into the air. While a few women and children did turn away, most in the gallery attentively watched

145

the carnage to follow. Sheriff Ramsey plunged the hammer into the top of Chris' skull. It made a sound like a cracking egg. He then did it again. And again. And again. He even spun the hammer around on several strikes, impaling the hammer claw into the soft flesh of Chris' face.

When he was finished, he stood up and started taking in quick, deep breaths. The Vaquero watched as the Sheriff's large belly moved rapidly up and down. Outside of being clothed, he looked like he had just finished having sex. When the Sheriff had finally caught his breath, he slowly walked over to face The Vaquero. Briefly looking down, The Vaquero thought he could see the remnants of an eyeball on one of the claw forks, just before it oozed off into the dirt. When he raised his gaze, the Sheriff was once again grinning from ear to ear. His face was spattered in blood and little tufts of scalp.

"I'm sorry you had to see that," said the Sheriff, sounding wholly sincere. The Vaquero stared and did not respond. "That's a mean stare. That's why you are a legend by God!" Sheriff Ramsey let out a meaty laugh and slapped The Vaquero on the shoulder. "Deputy Colson will walk you back to your horse. He'll tell you everything we know about the Cristo brothers. I think we've got a possible track on them. Bring those boys back to me. Dead or alive. But alive is better if you can. You've seen how we do things here. The people want their justice." The Vaquero stared blankly for another moment, then he stomached his disgust and tipped his hat. He made his way over to the deputy.

Deputy Colson did as ordered and gave The Vaquero all the information he knew on the Cristo brothers. It was short and sweet, but some of it quite informative. At this point, The Vaquero didn't really care what information he received. He'd take whatever leads he could get on the short walk back to his horse. Then he was getting the hell out of this bat shit crazy town. And that's just what he did.

Did he intend to hunt the Cristo Brothers? Yes. That was still his work. But he certainly wasn't bringing them back alive. He'd put them down and let someone else collect the bounty. He had no intention of ever visiting Chilicof again or spending any more quality time with the town's lunatic Sheriff.

5

A New Name

Thwack! The tip of Linius' knife bit into the soft flesh of a large white oak tree. Little splinters of bark sprayed out from the deepening hole. Linius had thrown the blade into that tree perhaps one hundred times and damn near hit the same spot on eighty of them.

He didn't hate being here. Or at least the physical nature of it. He enjoyed traversing the road. He enjoyed seeing new towns. He enjoyed meeting new people. He enjoyed sleeping under the stars and boiling coffee on a campfire. There was some danger, and he liked that too. He was built for it.

The part he didn't like was the company he had to keep. Linius Stallworth's asshole of a father, Herbert Stallworth, hadn't been present for the majority of his life. He'd been too busy soldiering to bother with raising a child. But now that Linius was seventeen, Herbert seemed to have a real stick up his ass about him becoming a soldier too.

Everyone acted like they respected Herbert. But Linius knew the truth. They feared him. And almost everyone had only seen the ugly side of Herbert. Linius had seen his ugly side's ugly side. He'd seen it in the form of his father's cold absence. Sometimes he saw it in his father's fists. Other times it was words he would hurl like weapons at his own family.

Whiff! Linius launched one of his throws way off the mark and sent his knife spiraling into the tall grass behind his target tree. He had to quit thinking about his old man. He had to quit thinking about the men he was stuck with. He needed to enjoy the good parts of this journey. The seeing new things. The meeting new people. Maybe doing some good in the world. Hell, he'd settle for just doing some good in Texas.

Linius Stallworth, at this time in 1867, was 2nd Lieutenant Linius Stallworth. He was one of six soldiers in private United States Army Division 415. This division was led by his father, Colonel Herbert Stallworth. The other men in the unit were all 1st Lieutenants. They outranked Linius, who was skilled with a weapon, but about as green of a soldier as you could be. They made sure to remind him of his rank at every opportunity. He found it odd; a colonel, leading this small battalion of low-ranking soldiers. But his father had told him their assignments were special. Whatever the hell that meant.

"The work we do is important, son." Linius thought of his father's words from last June. It was his recruitment speech. "You and I, we never had much time together, and before I knew it, you were grown. You got a man's body, but you are not a man yet. I'm going to bring you with me. Harden you. Bring you into the Stallworth legacy."

"How can you bring me into our legacy? Wasn't I born into our legacy?" Linius mumbled to himself as he stomped down tall swaths of grass whilst searching for his errant knife. "What is the Stallworth legacy for that matter? Being an asshole?" A small ray of sunlight shimmered on a partially concealed steel blade. It caught Linius' eye and he kneeled to retrieve his knife.

He gripped the smooth wooden hilt, appreciating the feel of the weapon in his hand. He thought for a moment the hilt was carved from white oak, just like the tree he was using for target practice. His father gave him this knife on his first day of joining the company. No, he didn't give it to him. He *issued* it to him. His father never really gave him anything except the occasional black eye and a red-faced ass chewing.

But recruitment Herbert had seemed different than Colonel Herbert or Father Herbert for that matter. He was still an asshole, but a little warmer maybe. Linius thought he likely confused that little bit of attention with compassion. But maybe that wasn't true. Was he being too hard on the old man? This was the only life he knew. Being a soldier. Being a tough guy. And now that his boy was of age, he wanted to make him a tough guy too. Teach him the ways of the sword and the gun.

"Linius!" Herbert called from the camp and he snapped out of his daze. He stood up in the tall grass, gave his trusted knife a smooth solitary flip in the air, then slipped it back into a leather holster on his left hip.

"Coming, sir!" He repressed childish thoughts and went back to being a soldier.

The entire troop was gathered around a modest campfire. Rory Swanson, probably the second biggest asshole in the unit, next only to Herbert Stallworth himself, was fixedly looking at Linius' knife.

"You throw that knife all the time because you can't shoot for shit or what?" Rory quipped.

"Nah, I don't even like knives that much. I'm only near perfect with the knife. But I *am* perfect with the gun." Linius patted the standard-issue revolver on his right hip.

"Bull shit!" Rory scoffed. The other 1st Lieutenants laughed in juvenile unison.

"Shut up. All of you." Herbert looked around the group, which quickly quieted down and stood at attention. "I believe we will arrive at our destination tomorrow and I'm going to need all of you to be focused."

"What's the directive, sir?" 2nd Lieutenant Rich Kauffer asked anxiously. Rich, like Linius and his father, was a black man. He was short, but built like a prize bull.

"Maybe if you'd shut the fuck up, I would tell you the directive?" Herbert, who towered over Rich, cut him a frustrated glare.

"Yes, sir. Sorry, sir."

"We are going into a refugee camp near the border of Mexico. As crazy as Commander Padillo is, he'd be a fucking madman to bring us any harm on Texas soil. But that being said, I never trust a Mexican. And we will be awfully close to the border."

Herbert spat on the ground in disgust. Linius knew of his people's early conflicts with Mexicans, but he didn't quite understand this animosity toward them. In those early days, it seemed as though black people had to conflict with nearly everyone in order to carve a place for themselves in the new world. He also knew that a small portion of Americans, including his father, wanted to annex Mexico and make a portion of its citizen's slave labor in the United States. Linius certainly didn't understand this concept at all. What could be more wrong than enslaving people against their will?

"Why is the President allowing Mexicans to camp on our side of the border, sir?" Rich asked eagerly. 2nd Lieutenant Clive Billings smacked him on the back of the head while Linius and Rory tried to stifle a laugh.

"What did I tell you to do, Rich?" Herbert scowled.

"You told me to shut the fuck up, sir."

"Next to my boy here, you are about the greenest son of a bitch I've ever had in my company. Are you sure you are a 2nd Lieutenant?"

"Yes, sir. It won't happen again, sir."

"It's my last warning, soldier."

"Yes, sir."

"Now, as I was saying. I never trust a Mexican. And especially a Mexican I am taking something from. President Johnson has seen fit to allow some of General Padillo's people refuge on our side of the border while he fights his civil war with General Esperanza. Personally, I could give a fuck who gets to be king of their shit hole country. But President Johnson has cozied up to Padillo and I am a soldier. What do soldiers do, 2nd Lieutenant Kauffer?" Rich, now too scared to speak, stared blankly at the Colonel. "Jesus Christ! When I don't want you to speak, I can't shut you the fuck up. But when I ask you a direct goddamn question the cat gets your tongue?" Herbert shook his head in disgust. "Linius! Boy! What do soldiers do?"

Linius arched his back to its most upright and attentive posture. "We take orders, sir!"

"Thank you, son. We take orders! And our orders are to enter this Mexican refugee camp and collect a supply wagon as compensation for President Johnson's kindness. This wagon should have several hundred pounds of gold and silver. It should also have four barrels of Tequila, which is perhaps the only thing Mexicans are good at making. We are to retrieve this payment and get it safely back to Fort Ruby."

151

Linius couldn't help but notice the lack of interest on Sam Walston's face. It was not a disrespectful disinterest. He just seemed to know all this already. Or perhaps he knew a little more than what was being said.

Although he was also a 2nd Lieutenant, Sam always came across as more seasoned than the other men. He was certainly Herbert's favorite. Rich, Clive, and Rory were mean, but in more of a childish way. Sam, on the other hand, was mean all the way through. Linius had only seen a taste of it, but he'd seen enough. It would not be shocking to find out his father had already briefed Sam on the mission. But now that Linius was really paying attention, Rory also looked like he knew some of this beforehand. Why were some of the men getting briefed before the others, and was there more information than what they were being told?

"Permission to speak, sir?" Linius asked his father.

"You see how that works, Rich?" Herbert paused. "Go ahead, son."

"Collecting, and then protecting a heavy payment in gold and silver. I get that. It's important. But it doesn't seem like our usual type of mission, sir. Is there something I'm missing?"

There was a touch of something on Herbert's face. It was either anger or pride. Linius wasn't sure which. "Linius, how long have you been with our troop?"

"A little over six months, sir."

"Six months. That's right. So, it would be safe to say that you don't know what our usual type of mission is. Would that be safe to say, son?"

Linius assumed he had angered the old man as usual and prepared himself to be chewed out, "Yes, sir."

"That's right. You don't know a goddamn thing about what we do." Herbert took in a deep breath. "However. Yes, there is a little more to this mission. Very perceptive of you, son. But that's on a need-to-know basis. And right now you don't need to know. Your mission is to ride into that refugee camp and do everything I tell you to do. Be professional. Be on guard. Be a 4-1-5 soldier. Can you do that?"

"Yes, sir."

"Good. At ease, men." The group started to disperse when Herbert put a hand on Linius' shoulder. "Not you. Take a walk with me, son."

Linius and his father strolled casually towards the white oak tree he had been using for target practice. Herbert reached out and rubbed the knife indentions with the pads of two fingers. Linius had once seen a blind man somehow reading by touching a series of bumps on paper. What had that been called? Braille maybe? His father touching the marks on the tree reminded him of this.

"You are good, son. With the knife." There was an unusual softness in Herbert's voice.

"Thank you, sir."

"You can cut the sir shit for now. We are just talking. Father and son." Linius didn't love this man. Not at all. But he did love the thought of having a father who wasn't a complete dick. It was hard not to be compelled by these rare moments of warmth.

"Thank you. I'm not bad with the knife. I throw it enough so I should be good. But I only throw it because I can't shoot the gun all the time. I love shooting."

"I'm one of the best goddamn shots I've ever seen. Sam and Rory aren't bad either. But you. My god. You are a marksman." Herbert gave an exceedingly rare smile and peered down at Linius. He appeared genuinely proud.

"It feels right. Holding that gun in my hand." The two men started walking further past the target tree. In the distance, a glowing orange sun dipped lower into the horizon.

"You were made to be a soldier, son. Stallworth's are soldiers. The finest officers. The best military bloodline this country has to offer."

"It's that part I don't know about. The soldier part."

"What are you going to do with that gun if you aren't a soldier? Shoot rabbits and squirrels? Rob banks?"

Linius laughed. "No, sir. I mean, No...Dad." He forced the word out of his mouth, fighting the urge to cringe.

"Your Mom. She made you a little soft. That's my fault. I should have been around more. I know that. I shouldn't have hit you when I was around. I know that too. But there's a lot of grit in you. It's in your blood. That's why I've brought you here. I'm hard on you, but I'm carving you into something you'll be proud of."

"I get it. I do. If being a soldier means I can make the world a better place. Protect our country. Help people. That's what I want to do."

A strange look came over Herbert's face. He looked like someone had died and he was going to break the news to a loved one. For the first time, Linius noticed the budding flecks of gray in his father's hair. "That is what soldiering is about, son. It is. But there are many ways you achieve those ends. Some of them are ugly. Some of them are not."

"Okay. So..." Linius sensed there was more, but he was a little confused.

"So we are a private division. Most of our missions are pretty straightforward. But sometimes we have missions that are more...off the record. Sometimes, they are ugly."

"Is that what this mission is?"

"Part of it will be, yes. And it will be hard. You are going to have to find some of that grit that's inside you." Herbert stopped walking and stared at the last orange fingers of sunlight flickering over the horizon.

"I'll find it. If we are doing the right thing." Linius looked up at his father who stared into the sunset.

After a long pause, Herbert finally spoke. "Head back now. Get some rest. We leave before first light."

***

They arrived at the Mexican refugee camp by noon the next day. Linius was familiar with the civil war ongoing in Mexico. He knew General Esperanza controlled much of southern Mexico and was pushing General Padillo and his people further and further North. He knew many Mexicans had been displaced from their towns or fled North before falling victim to General Esperanza's army. But until riding upon this camp, he had no idea of the scale of the conflict.

The camp was sprawling in size. There were thousands of people, with far fewer tents and makeshift buildings serving as shelters for them. The camp seemed to stretch east, west, and south for miles. Linius thought the camp must overlap both sides of the border. His heart sank, seeing this many people displaced from their homes. He didn't care if they were Mexican or not.

Colonel Stallworth and his men waited at the fringes of the refugee camp. They stood tall and still on horseback while a lone rider approached. As he got closer, Linius could see it was a short Mexican man. He looked thin, almost sickly, but he also looked energetic. The rider was still far away, but Linius could see there was a smile on his face as wide as the camp.

Rory was sitting near the front of the group when he turned to look back at the others. "This Mexican looks as silly on a horse as you do, Rich. He's like two feet tall."

Rich was pretty easy to get riled up if he was jabbed about his height and he responded quickly, "Do you think they have a doctor in this camp, Colonel? In case I have to beat the shit out of Rory?"

"I went to New York City once. As a kid. My pops took me to watch these horse races. All the riders were like that. Little midgets. Just like you and this Mexican. Maybe you two can have a race and we'll all place bets on you?"

"Shut up, Rory. Leave him alone." Linius was grateful not to be the one getting shit for a change, but he'd heard enough of this nonsense.

"What did you say to me, 1st Lieutenant?"

Colonel Herbert, who sat at the front of everyone and tolerated all he could, turned back to the group. "I will shoot every fucking one of you if you don't shut up. Act like you are soldiers in the 4-1-5. You hear me?"

"Yes, sir." All five men responded in unison as the jockey-statured Mexican approached.

"Hello! Hello! United States Army! So good we have you here!" The Mexican man greeted them with slightly broken English, but also a remarkably natural American accent. He leaped off his horse and eagerly approached each soldier, offering a handshake. "I am Carlos. I speak good English. I can translate for you on your visit. Yes?"

156

"Yes. I am Colonel Stallworth of the United States Army and these are my men. Are you in charge of the camp?"

"Me? Oh no! Oh no!" Carlos laughed. "Not in charge. Commander Miguel is in charge. He waits for you inside. We are very excited to welcome you. I am here to help. Anything you need."

"Very well. Take us to commander Miguel. We don't intend to be here long."

Carlos darted back to his dusty brown horse and effortlessly mounted the large animal, despite his small size and sickly appearance. "Si! Si! Yes! Yes! Follow me."

As the men rode deeper into the refugee camp, people gathered around them and watched with great interest. They didn't seem afraid. They looked grateful. Despite these poor living conditions, and undoubtedly little food, they were appreciative to be here. They were safe. Far away from General Esperanza and the conflict in their country.

As they rode deeper into the camp, the surrounding crowd became thicker. Their pace became slower. The path they followed was lined with hundreds of men, women, and children. They were smiling and waving, and several even shouted out *USA! USA! USA!* Linius thought this soldiering thing might not be too bad after all.

Children would dart across the road, laughing and gawking at the soldiers. Carlos would stop the group, playfully admonish the youngsters, then get everyone moving again. "They are really glad to see you. You let us stay on this beautiful land. They all say thank you."

Colonel Stallworth looked smug. "That's the American way, Carlos."

"Si! American Way!"

An elderly man, perhaps even shorter than Carlos (it was hard to tell from how badly he was hunched over) wandered into the middle of the road and once again stopped the group. "For fuck's sake," Herbert muttered under his breath. Carlos did not admonish this man. He paused and looked at him respectfully. The elderly man was wearing a white robe and several necklaces. He was adorned with brightly colored scarves and tassels. The scarves were different from what Linius had seen before. They were painted with intricate and colorful designs.

The elderly man said something in Spanish none of the men could understand. Carlos then turned back to explain. "This is P'aqo. He is our Chaman. You know this word?"

"He's your holy man," Sam answered.

"Si, yes, holy man. Chaman. He is respected here." Carlos paused, then looked directly at Linius. "He wants to know your name."

Linius was caught off guard. "My name?"

"Yes. Your name."

"Linius."

P'aqo scrunched up his old leathery face. He turned an ear towards Carlos.

"Linius!" Carlos shouted. The chaman moved closer to Carlos, who then leaned his ear down to his level. P'aqo spoke softly, too quietly for the other men to hear. It almost seemed as though they were arguing about something. Carlos raised back up on his horse and turned to Linius. He was blushing a little. "P'aqo says he will call you...Bringo."

Linius snickered and looked around at the other soldiers. They seemed to be enjoying this a great deal.

"What is a bringo?"

"P'aqo says you are black. And you are a gringo. So he call you Bringo." With the exception of the Colonel, all the other men found this hysterical and started laughing.

"What about him?" Linius chuckled, pointing to his father. "And him?" he pointed to Rich. "Aren't they bringos too?"

Carlos leaned over and seemed to translate this question to P'aqo. The old man responded by laughing and dismissively waving them away. Slowly, he stepped to the side and an embarrassed Carlos hurried the men on. As Linius passed by, P'aqo stared at him intently. His eyes were cloudy, almost milky, but incredibly intense. Linius tipped his hat and shook away the gooseflesh moving up his arms.

Soon the men came upon a clearing near the center of the camp. Linius figured they were nearly at the border of Mexico and perhaps already over it. The area they came upon was clear of tents and makeshift shelters, but there was a multitude of horses, some supply wagons, and a number of Mexican soldiers, all decked out in uniform.

Linius noticed that most of the soldiers, like the hundreds of refugees they encountered, were smiling. They looked grateful. Many of them were waving. A smaller number of them were saluting. One man stood out clearly amongst the others. He was undoubtedly Commander Miguel who had control over the encampment.

Commander Miguel was taller than most of the Mexican soldiers. He was also older, with short greying hair and a thick white mustache. He was wearing the dark blue suit of a Mexican officer. Large gold buttons ran up the center of his jacket. On his shoulders were large gold pads, which dangled with even more gold frills. His medals were only on his left side and ran from nearly his waistline up to his collarbone. Linius, nor any of the other men, had ever seen a soldier so ornately decorated.

"Welcome!" Commander Miguel shouted, and saluted the unit. Colonel Stallworth and his men all saluted back. "I speak some English. But it is poor. You please forgive me."

"Esta Bien," said Colonel Stallworth. Linius was caught off guard, not realizing his father knew any Spanish.

"You speak Spanish?" he quietly asked his father.

"Very little. Just a few pleasantries." Herbert was speaking low, then elevated his voice. "Commander Miguel, si?"

The man nodded in agreement and pounded lightly on his chest. "Commander Miguel."

Herbert crossed one arm over his own chest. "Colonel Stallworth." He then pointed at his men, one by one. "2nd Lieutenants Sam, Rory, Rich, and Clive."

The Commander looked puzzled for a moment. He pointed a finger at the only soldier left unnamed. "Quien es?"

Herbert, completely straight-faced, replied, "1st Lieutenant Bringo."

All the men, with the exception of himself, laughed hysterically at this. Clive damn-near fell off his horse. Even Commander Miguel and several of his men were laughing, although they weren't sure why. This humorous moment seemed to put everyone at ease.

"In all seriousness, Commander, you know why we are here. The United States has allowed your refugee camp to encroach North into American soil. In exchange, you have agreed to make payments of precious metals. Per the communication I received, you will have a wagon ready for us which we can transport back."

Commander Miguel looked at Carlos, who immediately began translating into Spanish. Commander Miguel was nodding his head in agreement, then replied in their native tongue.

Carlos looked back to Colonel Stallworth. "Commander Miguel says your payment is prepared. We pay America with honor. The wagon is secure several miles away from camp. He will send his men for it immediately. Right away. It will be here by morning."

"Tell him we'd like to leave at first light. I'd prefer the wagon here tonight, so we can leave in the morning without delay." Linius didn't like a lot of things about his father, but he could respect the way he commanded a situation. His voice had a way of compelling people to comply.

Carlos nodded and began speaking to the Commander again. They shared a short exchange. "The commander says yes. He will have the wagon to you tonight. It can be secured to your horses so you leave with no delay at morning. He will post men to guard the wagon so you get good sleep."

"We appreciate that. But I always have my men on post. We can keep our own eyes on the wagon."

More words were translated back and forth between Carlos and the Commander. "The commander says as you wish. He is at your service if needed. One more thing, Colonel?"

"What's that?"

"The commander would like to invite you to dinner tonight to honor your men. Honor United States. Would be our pleasure."

"My boys do love to eat. We will happily attend."

There was another translated exchange between the Commander and Colonel, but something else caught Linius' attention and drew him away from the conversation. He noticed Sam had become disengaged from what was going on. He was scanning the camp, looking for something. Perhaps he was just being cautious. But Linius didn't think so.

The men were given comfortable quarters in some well-built tents a little further south, but still well within the camp. Almost all the men took a mid-afternoon nap, or *siesta* as Clive jokingly called it. Even the Colonel slept briefly. Only Sam seemed to stay awake and vigilant the entire time.

When they were summoned out later that night, they were surprised to find the same camp center where they met with Commander Miguel had been turned into a festival ground. Long wooden tables, perhaps a dozen of them, were lined up in neat rows. There were multiple fire pits and spits all around cooking food that smelled delicious. If there was one thing the soldier life offered little of, it was good food on the road. All of their stomachs grumbled with anticipation.

Some women in the camp were stringing colorful fabric between many of the tents. It reminded Linius of the scarves worn by P'aqo. Many of the women were also dressed in decorative and colorful clothing. He assumed these were all traditional symbols of celebration and he found the culture here endearing.

"All this for us?" he asked his father.

"I presume so."

"That's pretty amazing."

"Don't drop your guard."

"I won't."

"And this goes for all of you." The Colonel pulled his men in tight. "I don't care how bad you want it, no Tequila. No booze of any kind. You drink their dirty Mexican water and stay sober. You understand?"

162

"Yes, sir," they said in unison, their voices tinged with disappointment.

"Get those pitiful looks off your faces. We are here on a mission," Sam interjected unexpectedly and with aggression in his voice. Sam only outranked Linius, but they all seemed to forget that for a moment.

"Yes, sir!" the men repeated in unison, only this time with a lot more compliance in their voices.

"Good. Now go have a little fun. Sam, you stay with me." The Colonel clapped Sam on the shoulder and the men went their separate ways.

Later that night, Linius found himself sitting at one of the long dinner tables. Carlos was seated next to him and the rest of the table was filled with Mexican men and women he didn't know and couldn't understand. But he couldn't be happier. There were sweet smells all around him in the cool night air. His belly was full to bursting. It was his first time eating something called enchiladas, and he loved them. He was offered tequila about two dozen times that night, but he somehow managed to refrain. The night couldn't be much nicer. Neither could the people.

Linius felt a small tap on his knee. He looked down to see an adorable little Mexican girl. She was maybe five or six years old. She had long, coal-black hair and eyes as big as dinner plates. She held up the little hand she had been tapping Linius with and gave him a heart-melting wave.

"Well, hello there. What is your name?"

Before she could reply, if she even understood him, a slightly older boy came up behind her. He grabbed her shoulder and scolded her in Spanish. "Lo siento! Lo siento!".

"It's okay. It's okay, really." Linius held up his hands and tried to make the boy feel at ease. He couldn't have been much older than the little girl. Maybe eight or nine years old. But he was doing his best to look after her like a parent. After a few moments, all seemed to be okay and the two children ran away, playing.

"They are brother, sister."

"I thought so. Cute kids."

"Si. Yes. Very cute. They are..." Carlos thought hard for a moment, trying to come up with the word. "...orphans."

"That's terrible to hear. From the conflict, with General Esperanza?"

"Yes."

"Who watches over them?"

"We do."

"We, as in you?" Linius pointed to Carlos.

"Me, yes. But all of us." Carlos motioned in a circle around the camp. "Their parents killed in war. So we all take them in. They stay mostly with senorita Claudia. She is old. Her husband was killed in war also. So she likes having the kids around."

"That's kind of her. Kind of all of you. You have something special here, with your people and this community."

"I think you have good heart too, Bringo."

Linius laughed. "I think that nickname is going to stick with me."

Carlos pointed a few tables down. "He always gives name. I am sorry."

Linius was surprised to see P'aqo sitting just a few tables down. If he'd been there most of the night, Linius hadn't noticed him at all until now.

164

"It's okay. Don't be sorry."

"Si. I am very drunk. I will go to bed now."

Linius chuckled. "I'm not drunk, but bed is probably best for me too."

Soon after finishing his conversation with Carlos, Linius was laying in his tent, still enjoying his full stomach. The wind had picked up and it ruffled the fabric of their large tent. All the men in the unit had come back at roughly the same time. When Linius arrived, Herbert and Sam had already hitched a large yellow wagon to two of their horses. The horses were then secured to a post outside their tent and ready to leave at first light.

Rory and Clive's horses would be pulling the wagon, so they agreed to ride the wagon out. Riding horseback was a kind of uncomfortable you got used to, but the small wooden bench seat on top of the wagon looked completely miserable. As annoying as they were, Linius felt bad for them drawing the short straw on that one. The Colonel had designated Sam to keep watch during the night. Something he seemed more than eager to do. Linius still felt something was up with Sam, and maybe Rory, so he decided he'd try to stay awake himself. But the past few weeks of miles traveled, and the heavy enchiladas in his stomach became too much. He drifted off quickly and didn't wake again until just before sunrise.

"Wake up, son. Time to go. Quick." The Colonel gave Linius a hard shake.

"Yes, sir." Linius' soldier conditioning kicked in and he popped out of bed. "Is there a problem?"

"No problem. Just move your ass." Despite the reassurance, his father certainly seemed on edge. Linius noticed all the other men were awake and looked like they had been for a while. Had he missed something? He was suspicious and also sad to go, but he saddled up and prepared to ride out with his troop. The first hints of sunlight were coming up in the eastern sky and a faint crescent moon hung over their heads.

The men had telegraphed their intentions to leave at first light, so their exit raised no suspicion. They passed a few Mexican soldiers who patrolled the camp, but they were confronted with nothing more than polite waves and salutes. Most of the refugees were still sleeping, but Linius saw several were up and already working outside their shelters to prepare for the day. He felt these were hard-working and good people.

The men traveled dozens of miles before anyone even spoke a word. Linius didn't understand the silence, he just accepted it. The air around them felt heavy, but most of the tension from the morning was gone. Whatever the mission was. Whatever danger they might have been in. His father seemed to feel it had passed.

"I reckon we are far enough into Texas I can take a leak now," Sam called back from his horse.

"Yeah, this should be good. Over there." The Colonel pointed to a small path leading off the main trail. It looked narrow and rough, but it was just wide enough for the wagon. It cut through a thick grove of trees and the thought of shade sounded great. It was turning out to be one hell of a hot day. Rory and Clive on top of the wagon were surely taking the worst of it. Linius thought they might have to peel their testicles off the riding bench when they stood up.

The narrow path made a brief jaunt through the thick trees, then turned sharply and led down to the bank of a large creek. There was plenty of room to spread out. They could tie the horses up and get the wagon turned around when they were ready to get back on the road. Did they find this spot by chance, or did Sam and the Colonel already know about it?

The men settled in for a quick break and Linius followed Sam over to some bushes to relieve his bladder. They pissed, side-

166

by-side, for what seemed like an eternity, and that was when Linius noticed something peculiar. There was a small swatch of blood smeared down Sam's right cheek.

"What's that on your face?" Linius asked, as the two men continued to make water.

"What?"

"On your face. Looks like dried blood." Sam touched his left cheek. "No, other side," Linius said.

Sam felt his right cheek for a moment. He looked at his fingers and saw nothing. So he licked his thumb and wiped his cheek again. This time, he could see a red stain on the soft white pad of his finger. "I'll be damned. Guess it is blood."

"Who's blood is it?"

"You ask a lot of fucking questions." Sam shook some final dribbles of piss and rebuttoned his pants.

Linius, also fastening his pants, pushed on. "I just want to know whose blood it is. That's all. Why would you have blood on you?"

"Why don't you ask your father?"

"I will." Linius increased his pace and made a sharp cut over to his father. "Colonel. Sir. Sam has blood on his face and I'd like to know why."

All the men stopped what they were doing and watched the unfolding scene. But again, they didn't seem clueless as to what was taking place. Linius grew more and more confident the only soldier in the dark was him.

Herbert stared at his son for a moment. He was silent, contemplative. And mean. He looked downright mean. All at once, it was like he reached some momentous decision. "Alright, it's time. Go on. Show him, Sam."

Sam walked to the back of the wagon with a smug grin on his face. The men all watched as Sam unbound the leather strappings to the wagon's cargo hold.

"Let's see. I better take an inventory of this wagon. Several heavy-ass gold bars. Even more heavy-ass silver bars. Some kind of weird spices and shit. Four barrels of the world's finest tequila." His smug grin then turned into a delighted smile. "Oh, and two little Mexican dogs."

Sam reached into the wagon and yanked out a bound and gagged little boy, and then an even smaller bound and gagged little girl. He threw them to the dirt, and they whimpered as they hit the hard ground. Linius was horrified to see it was the orphan brother and sister he met at last night's celebration.

He rushed over to the children and knelt to console them. "What the hell? What is this? Are you okay, kids? Uhm...Lo siento! Lo siento!"

"Stand up, son. Stand up and get over here!" the Colonel yelled. Linius had heard that tone many times before a beating.

He stood up, nose to nose with Sam for a moment, then slowly backed up towards his father. "Fuck you." He pointed an angry finger at Sam. "Fuck all of you." He looked around. "Did you all know about this?"

Herbert closed the distance between them with the speed of a predatory cat, and struck him with an open hand. It wasn't a particularly hard slap, but enough to get Linius' attention. He stared his father down, panting rapidly and tears welling up in his eyes.

"Listen to me, boy. Calm yourself down and I'll explain to you what is going on."

"Yes, sir," he replied through clenched teeth.

"General Padillo made an agreement to pay our nation stipends and treasure if we allowed refugee camps on American soil. He also agreed to cease all trade with the French. He's come through well-enough on the treasure, but he has continued to defy the embargo with France. He is paying them three times in gold what we are getting."

"Why would he do that? They were so grateful to us." Linius asked, angry and confused.

"The French are supplying him with weapons. That's more important to him. We give him our own precious soil and he insults us. Defies us. It could not be tolerated."

"What do these two orphans have to do with any of that?"

All the men laughed at this. "They aren't orphans, man," Rich said before realizing he was speaking out of turn. "Sorry for interrupting, sir."

The Colonel didn't scold Rich this time. "He's right, Linius. They aren't orphans. Those two little Mexicans are General Padillo's children. He hid them away in that camp to keep them out of harm's way." There was a long pause. "But we are harm's way, son."

"We are going to hurt little kids to get back at the general?" Linius looked around at everyone in genuine disbelief at what he was hearing.

"Bring them over here. All of them," Herbert said, walking away toward a large cargo chest resting on the ground. Rory, Clive, and Rich circled around Linius, redirecting him to his father.

"Get your fucking hands off me!" he shouted, jerking himself away from them. "Just take care of the kids. Don't let that mother fucker Sam grab them."

Sam laughed callously at this. "I'm flattered. You think I'm the big bad wolf or something?"

Rory brought the little boy over to the chest and pushed him down to his knees. The boy placed his elbows on the chest, holding his bound hands up in a praying position. The Colonel removed a knife from his belt, one nearly identical to Linius', and placed it on the chest to the boy's side. He then removed his service pistol and placed it on the other side. All the men gathered in front of the chest. The little girl, who looked truly terrified, was standing in front of Rory and Clive, restrained by their heavy grip on her shoulders.

"What the hell is this, Dad?" Linius felt like he was in an awful dream. Whatever was happening here, none of it was right. He didn't sign up for anything like this. This was not in the recruitment speech.

"Just come here, son."

Linius approached his father's side. They were both standing behind the young boy.

"Take a breath."

He tried, but it felt like his lungs were filled with hot ash. He did manage to slow his pulse and start to think rationally about the situation.

"Mexicans aren't people. They aren't human beings. They are more like wild animals. You get some butterflies in your stomach because their old witch gives you a funny nickname, and suddenly you think these savages are just like us. But all the while they are double-dealing behind our back. Behind your back. Our country did them a great kindness and they spit on our generosity. Sometimes wild animals have to be broken. They have to be taught lessons."

"I...I..." Linius tried to speak.

170

"When my father and my father's father came over to this land. You think it was easy? You think the white man, who outnumbered us, just gave us a seat at the table? Hell no. We earned our place at the table. Because we were hard men. Mexican trash like this and fucking savage Indians did nothing but get in our way. But we overcame them. We are Stallworths. We are a legacy."

Linius looked down at the weapons beside the boy. "What do you want me to do?"

"You are going to kill this wild animal. By the blade or the bullet. Your choice. But this is where you find your grit. This is when you toughen up and become a soldier. Even though right now you think this is ugly, you are still going to find the strength to do it."

"And if I don't?"

"All your friends here have been on the road a long time. Like all men they have needs. I think they are going to have a little fun with that tiny piece of ass they're holding. And if you don't kill this little boy, I'm going to make him watch what they do to his sister. You want that on your conscience?"

Linius was in pure shock at the words coming out of his father's mouth. He looked at each soldier and saw in their faces they intended to do it. Clive was actually rubbing his crotch in anticipation. Rich, maybe just Rich, showed some hesitation in his eyes. How could Linius have spent the past six months with such poisonous men and not know they were this barbaric?

But through his shock and disgust, other parts of him were waking up. His eyes had dried, his breath had calmed, and his pulse had slowed to a crawl. His vision changed. It grew sharper. He could hear the soft babble of the creek and the crackling of leaves blowing in the light breeze. He thought for a moment he could hear the heartbeat of the little boy in front of him.

He reached down and grabbed the seven-inch blade with the white oak handle. It was like his, but not quite. It didn't fit as comfortably in his palm, but he thought he could still wield it well. He gripped the boy's forehead and tilted his head back to expose a vulnerable neck. He slowly moved the knife behind the boy's arms and rested the blade right on the child's adam's apple.

"That's right. Time to become a man. To become a soldier." The Colonel might as well have been a little red devil sitting on Linius' shoulder, spitting venom into his ear.

Linius feigned a shaking hand. "I don't know that I can do this, sir."

"You can do it. You will do it. It's hard miles to become a man. The tragedies are what shapes us. The road is what changes us. And these are the ends that find us. When you slit that boy's throat. Then, and only then, have you truly started your journey."

"Then let's begin," Linius said coldly.

He gave the knife a quick single flip in the air and caught it by the blade. With lightning speed, he lunged it into Sam's throat. It was much softer than the white oak target tree, and it split open like a piece of firewood. Blood sprayed out in a crimson arch and left a dripping red line down Herbert's face.

Before Sam's body had dropped to the ground, Linius had already retrieved the pistol from the other side of the chest. He made two quick shots and left a dark blue bullet hole between both Clive and Rory's eyes. They had barely touched the handle of their guns before he sent their brains flying out the back of their skulls. All three men dropped to the ground with a lifeless thud. The little girl, now free of their gripping hands, fell down and curled up in a tight ball.

Herbert found himself frozen, speechless, and unarmed. He watched as Linius took a few steps back and trained the pistol on Rich, whose right hand was flirting above his sidearm.

"I really don't want to kill you, Rich. You didn't want to be a part of all this, did you?"

"Shoot him, Rich," Herbert commanded after finding his voice again.

Rich's eyes shot back and forth between Herbert and Linius.

"I'm too fast, Rich. You don't have a chance. Don't do this."

"You *can* shoot him and you *will* shoot him, Lieutenant. That is an order. He is a traitor to our country. He has murdered, in cold blood, our fellow soldiers. It is your duty to shoot him."

Linius could see the slight change in Rich's eyes and knew that Herbert's authority was beating away at his common sense. "Please," Linius mouthed.

"Now!" Herbert screamed!

Rich clutched the handle of his gun, but never stood a chance to draw it. Linius fired a third shot from his father's gun and watched the bullet explode through Rich's left eyeball. The man's body went limp and he tumbled to the ground, landing on Clive's twitching corpse.

Linius then turned and trained the gun on his father. Herbert's face was pulled tight in a snarl and he was breathing heavily through his nose. "You are a traitor. You are not my son. You are not a Stallworth. You hear me? You are not part of our legacy! You are a weak, spineless pussy poisoned by your mother!"

"Fuck your name. I'll just go by Bringo."

Linius fired a fourth and final shot. Herbert's skull split down the middle, and meaty chunks of grey brain matter splattered onto the oak tree behind him. He dropped first to his knees, then fell forward flat on his face. Or at least, what was left of his face.

Linius had felt in complete control when all the shooting started. But now that it was over, everything started to spin. He dropped to one knee and tried to steady the dizziness in his brain. Remembering the two young children brought the world back into focus.

He cut them loose and cleaned them up. They were terrified. But not scared of him. In fact, both children hugged him when their hands and feet were free. They sat quietly on top of the wagon while Linius worked to clean up the mess he made.

He dragged the bodies into a shallow creek. He thought moving his father's corpse might give him some remorse, but he didn't feel a thing. It seems his father had hardened him up after all, just not in the way he intended.

He lowered the children off the wagon and had the horses drag it as close to the creek bank as possible. He then freed them of their load and swatted their rears, sending them running into the thick trees.

There was an axe in one of their supply bags and he was able to break off one of the wagon's long tongues. He used it, as a lever of sorts, to position under the wagon's bolster and tip it sideways into the creek. Despite the good leverage, it was a difficult task. Luckily, the wagon had come to rest on a slight slope that ran down into the creek bank.

Linius freed all the remaining horses but his own. He saddled up and positioned both children in front of him. Then they rode a hot and hard twenty-three miles back south. Two miles from the refugee camp, his horse's front leg fell into an obscured gopher hole and snapped. As one final act of horror for the day, Linius had to shoot his horse in the head. He held hands with both children at his side and they made the last two miles on foot.

He didn't know what to expect when he arrived back at camp. He figured Sam had murdered senorita Claudia and taken the children during the night. It may be him that would hang for the murder. If so, he was resigned to it. In his heart, he just wanted to get the children back home.

As they came into the camp, a crowd had gathered at the front. Commander Miguel stood ahead of everyone. Carlos was also there at his side. There were many refugees, but also many soldiers, and Linius thought for certain he'd be killed.

Commander Miguel stepped forward and knelt to the ground. The children let go of Linius' hands and raced into the Commander's arms. Then some women from the camp raced over and shuffled them away to safety. But before she could be taken away and tended to, the little girl darted back over to Linius and gave him one final (and gigantic) hug. Even if he were to die, Linius thought that hug would carry him nicely into the afterlife.

"What happened, senor?" Carlos asked.

Linius' throat felt like it was coated in sand, and every muscle in his body ached. But he stood tall and spoke the truth. "The men I was with. They were bad men. I didn't know what they did. What they intended to do. When I found out, I stopped them. I'm sorry if anyone was hurt because of them."

Carlos looked around at the crowd and spoke in Spanish. Many people were speaking back, but Linius couldn't understand what they were saying.

"Thank you. Thank you for doing the right thing," Carlos said softly. Linius watched as the commander nodded his head in agreement. The others who had gathered around all seemed to share the same sentiment. Once again, he found his eyes welling up with tears.

From the crowd, P'aqo slowly hobbled forward. At a snail's pace, he made his way over to Linius and spoke to him. He couldn't understand P'aqo's words, but he could feel the brevity in his voice.

"P'aqo says you are not a bringo. You were never a bringo. You are not a soldier either and you'll never be a soldier. P'aqo says you are Vaquero. You are *The Vaquero*."

"What is a vaquero?" Linius' knees felt as though they might buckle.

"A vaquero is like an American Cowboy. But P'aqo says you are The Vaquero. A special title. *The Vaquero* stops bad men. Brings them to justice."

Minutes earlier, he thought he would surely be imprisoned or killed, but now felt like he was being knighted by this mystical holy man. Linius, who would be known as The Vaquero for the rest of his days, felt the weight of this title. It felt good bringing bad men to justice. Even if one of them had been his father. It felt good saving the children from the clutches of evil men. If that were to be his path, it was one he'd proudly ride.

"Thank you."

"Si Vaquero. You must go. You must go. You won't be safe here. If anyone comes asking questions, we don't say you ever came back. Si?"

"Si."

Commander Miguel did as Carlos said and gave The Vaquero a horse. He rode away into the night and arrived at Fort Ruby two weeks later. He explained to the commanding officers that the 4-1-5 were ambushed while returning to Fort Ruby, robbed of the wagon, and all of his companions killed. He had barely escaped with his life, thanks only to a brave act of heroism by his father. It made him sick to tell this glorifying lie, but he thought it was best to sell his story and bring his mother some comfort.

The bodies of the private army division 415 were never discovered. The wagon and its load were never retrieved. By American forces anyway. Herbert Stallworth was posthumously awarded a medal of valor based on his son's account of the events that unfolded. The Vaquero was made to serve another three years in the United States Army, thankfully on less dark operations and

177

more standard military affairs. During those three years, his mother passed away to cancer at the young age of forty-eight.

After his honorable discharge in 1871, and with no family to care for, The Vaquero took to the road, completely abandoning his given name and any connection to his previous life. He started picking up bounties and ended up making quite a name for himself. He would become known as a relentless bounty hunter, who more often than not brought his tickets in cold.

Near the end of his bounty hunting career, he'd find himself on the trail of two murderous brothers. They had killed two children not much different in age than General Padillo's. It made him think of his time in Texas and how he earned his name. There was nothing worse than a child-killer and he'd be eager to bring them to justice. But he couldn't help but feel he was also chasing something else. In a seedy hotel and saloon in Gallows, Missouri, he'd finally find out what it was.

6

Welcome To Gallows

The blade of an axe dug its way into the meat of a large tree stump. It made a loud *thunk* and startled John Robinson awake. Was that right? Had he been sleeping? More like zoned out. Daydreaming. Just no dreams this time.

"Both racks here are loaded, and the big one out back too. I'm done splitting trees for the night," a large, imposing man called over to the bartender.

"Stays this busy I might need your services again tomorrow," the bartender, also a notably large and imposing figure called back.

The burly wood splitter let go of the axe and turned to John with a mischievous grin. "He keeps me splitting this much wood and I'll be upping my prices," he said in a low voice, then headed for the door. There's always a little more truth to be told in banter, but the exchange between all the men was friendly enough.

John's table was adjacent to a large fireplace in the back of the saloon. The space in front of the fireplace was mostly empty, albeit for a large wooden stump, which made for an axe holder and a decorative piece of sorts. It gave the otherwise modern saloon a rustic accent. Two good size iron racks were on either side of the fireplace and both were neatly stocked with split logs.

The bartender wasn't joking about being busy. John was damn near the only customer when he dozed off. Now he was one of the lucky few patrons to have a table. It couldn't have been much later than noon when he left his hotel room above the bar. His thoughts felt like they had been stuffed with cotton. What time was it? How long had he been down there and how much did he have to drink? There was booze in his blood. He could feel it. But he felt another type of intoxication. It didn't escape him that this was likely the work of the glioblastoma.

"Saving these chairs for anyone?" A tall man approached. John looked up, and although things were a little blurry, he knew he didn't favor the man's eyes. They were wild eyes. He was accompanied by a shorter, good-looking man who appeared frazzled and withdrawn.

John looked across his table and saw two empty chairs. "I was saving them for you two fine gentlemen." He reached for a shot glass, intending to make a toasting gesture, but he found it empty.

"It appears I have run low on spirits. Please, sit, and I will correct this right away."

The two men cut each other a humored look and took their seats at John's table. "Standing room only in here. Appreciate you sharing the seats. Name's Jamie." The taller man reached out his hand.

"John. Nice to meet you, Jamie. And you're welcome." He reached out and his hand showed a noticeable tremble. As they shook hands, his eyes shifted over to Jamie's companion, who was looking down into his lap. "And you are, young man?"

The man didn't seem to recognize someone was speaking to him. "Dusty," Jamie cut in and spoke for him. "You'll have to forgive him. He's been a little under the weather."

"Hate to hear it. Can he drink?"

"How about it, Dusty? Can you drink?" Jamie gave him a hard slap on his back.

Dusty started to speak, but all that came out was a raspy scraping sound. He cleared his throat, swallowed, and tried again. "Yes, I'll take a drink." His eyes glanced up and met John's for the first time. John didn't care for Dusty's eyes either, but they didn't have the same feral quality as Jamie's.

"Very well then." John let an ear-piercing whistle and raised a hand into the air. An attractive young woman in a frilly white two-piece pajama set approached the table.

"Still with us I see, Mr. Robinson. You ready to start again?" she asked, while collecting the empty shot glass and adding it to the growing collection on her tray.

"Oh yes. Shots for me and my friends. This is Jamie, and Dusty." Both men gave an awkward nod.

"You got it. Whiskey comin' up, Mr. Robinson," the barmaid said and darted away as quickly as she had appeared.

"I reckon she has a couple different jobs around here." Jamie licked his lower lip.

"I reckon she might," John said flatly and again found himself assessing Jamie's eyes.

"Is this a, you know, brothel?" The man questioned. "My brother and I, we haven't ever been here before. To Gallows."

"I've spent a little time on the road. This is one of the nicer hotel and saloon setups I've ever visited. I'm sure that business goeson here, but they don't advertise it. I think they are trying to keep this place a little more upscale."

"Well, for fuck's sake. Gallows seems pretty big, but it ain't like its Kansas City."

John didn't have a chance to reply before the barmaid returned and sat down three tall shots of whiskey.

Round 1

John looked over to the bar and read the large words painted above it. There was a black cowboy standing there, whose hat was so big it nearly covered up the bottom of the letters. But John could still make them out clearly. *Welcome To Gallows*. It wasn't his first time visiting Gallows. Nor was it his first time at the hotel and bar. But for the life of him, he couldn't remember *why* he was there. If he chased a demon, he thought it might only be the one in the shot glass.

"Brothers, did you say?" John tried to shake the cobwebs from his mind with a little more conversation.

"Yeah. Brothers. Passing through town on our way to a job in Coffey." Jamie's words came out like an actor reading a script for the first time.

182

"Cheers then. To work." John raised his glass and the men toasted. Even Dusty, who looked sullen and sickly, raised his glass then tipped back the shot.

John's whistle cut through the room again. "One more please!" He raised his hand and pointed at their small wooden table. The empty glasses were taken away and replaced with three more shots, so full they nearly spilled over the brim.

Round 2

"Been pretty chilly the past couple of nights. I think you got the best table in the house next to this fire. Nothing better to warm your bones than a little whiskey and a nice fire. That and a little pussy." As if on cue, the roaring fireplace behind the men crackled and burped out a large *pop.*

"Can't argue that. I love a good fire. Whiskey and fire ain't bad when you got a fever too." John looked over to Dusty.

"Ain't got no fever. Just don't feel good, that's all," the man muttered.

Jamie looked at his brother the way a parent might look at their child, waiting for them to misbehave or say something inappropriate. "Too much time on the road," Jamie interjected, "A roof over his head tonight will have him right as rain. Ain't that right, Dusty?"

The man rolled his eyes upward as if to inspect his own thoughts. "Right as rain?" he pondered, then nodded and giggled strangely. "Yeah, that's right. Right as rain."

A tension seemed to form between the two men. John made the decision to cut it. "Alright then. So this one is to a good fire, some good whiskey..." John's eyes cut over to Jamie. "...And a little pussy! Eh' Jamie?"

"To pussy!" Jamie echoed and clanged his glass against John's.

"Right as rain," Dusty muttered and toasted his shot as well.

The whiskey went down. John whistled. The barmaid in frilly white pajamas replaced the shots yet again.

Round 3

"I'm having a good time and all, mister. Don't want you to take no offense. But we've got a long trip ahead of us. Not sure I want to spend all our money on devil water," Jamie said, while picking up another full shot of whiskey.

John reached into the inner pocket of his black jacket and revealed a black cloth bag. It was tied off at the top with a little gold piece of cord. He shook the bag, making a loud and unmistakable sound of coins clanging together. "No worries boys. The spirits are on me tonight. Consider it compensation for your good company and conversation."

The two men exchanged a glance. "Well, if those coins are burning a hole in your pocket. Then consider us hired." Jamie tipped back the third shot of whiskey and slammed the empty glass back down.

John tipped his back as well, but placed his empty glass down with much less authority. "You done drinking, Dusty?" John asked with his eyes fixed on Jamie.

"Not by a long shot," Dusty said, and downed the only remaining shot on the table.

Round 4

"A little reckless, wouldn't you say?" Jamie questioned John.

"What's that?"

184

"Flashing your money around like that. Seems like a lot of change to be advertising in this packed bar."

"Yeah, could be. But you've got to think about the psychology of it. I figure there's a couple reasons a man like me might wave around his money like that." John was staring affectionately at his fourth shot.

"Well please, elaborate." Jamie's tone was starting to show more of his true color.

"Some men may just not know better. Maybe they came into a lot of money and it makes them feel big. So they wave it around to feel good about themselves."

"Good way to get your teeth kicked in." Jamie was quick to point out, and John was confident Jamie had delivered some of those teeth-kickings a time or two.

"Ain't that the truth. Those men either learn their lesson, or eventually they end up broke, or dead, or both." There was a hefty pause while John seemed to organize his thoughts. "Then other men..." he continued. "...Other men aren't scared to show their money. They think they are the meanest son of a bitch around. They don't think anyone who sees that money will be man enough to take it from them."

"Those men usually end up broke, or dead, or both also. There's always someone bigger. Someone tougher. Wouldn't you say, John?"

"Most of them. Yeah. But some of them really are the meanest sons of bitches in the room. And they don't lose a red cent."

"Is that you, John? You the meanest son of a bitch in the room?" Jamie continued, verbally puffing out his chest.

"You can put your dick away, Jamie. I'm not trying to get your hackles up. My situation, my psychology, is different from both of those. But first..." John raised his shot glass. "To the meanest sons of bitches in the room." The three men toasted and the barmaid replenished their round again.

Round 5

"You were saying. Your situation is different?" Some of the aggression in Jamie's voice had diminished.

"Ahh yes. My situation. I'm the man with nothing to lose."

"How so?" Jamie was still doing all the talking, but Dusty was noticeably taking more interest in the conversation now. He was also getting more noticeably unsteady in his seat.

"I'm dying," John stated without emotion.

"Dying?"

"Yes, dying. Something is wrong in here." He wrapped his knuckles on the side of his skull. "My doctor tells me I don't have very long." He had never spoken to a doctor, but thought of his dead brother Jerry dressed up in an oversized white coat and holding a stethoscope. He let out a small laugh.

"You're about to take a dirt nap and you're laughing about it?"

"Just thinking about something else. But yeah, you get used to the idea after a while. Things like taking out my little coin bag in the middle of this bar don't seem to matter much anymore."

"Dying or not, it's still a good way to get the shit kicked out of you."

"It's a funny thing. I remember the first time I did get the shit kicked out of me on the road. And robbed. It was before I knew about this." He wrapped the side of his skull again.

186

"But here you are still flashing your money around?" Jamie almost seemed agitated at John's stupidity.

"Well, I've spent a lot of time on the road since then. I'm not the meanest son of a bitch in the room. But I can handle myself in most situations. I expect I'll be six feet deep by the end of the month. So who really gives a fuck, you know? If I want to take out my little bag of coins, I'm going to do so."

"Yeah." Jamie tipped back his fifth shot. "Who really gives a fuck?" Two more shots went down the hatch and the sixth round made its way to the table.

Round 6

"Before my time on the road. I was a banker. Can you believe that?"

"You don't strike me as a banker. I'll say that. At least until you start pulling those money bags out of your jacket."

"Oh, that's nothing."

"Say again?" The noise in the bar had picked up and Jamie was struggling to hear.

John raised his voice a few notches. "I said that's nothing. I've got a ton of money up in my room."

"You don't say?" Jamie looked over to Dusty, who was fixedly watching John.

"I think it's us," Dusty said, almost inaudibly.

"Say again? Speak up, son," John replied.

"I think it's us," he said, louder this time. "I think we are the meanest sons a bitches in the room. Maybe in the whole town."

"Shut the fuck up, Dusty," Jamie scolded.

"My brother is at least. He's one of the meanest you'll ever meet," Dusty continued, despite his brother's glaring eyes.

Jamie took a deep, calming breath. "I said shut up, Dwaine."

"Dwaine? I thought his name was Dusty?" John chimed in. His words were starting to slur and his face was drooping.

Jamie thought carefully before replying. "Look, John. I'm gonna cut you straight."

"Please do." John downed his shot, and Dwaine promptly followed. Jamie, however, left his on the table.

"We are bad men. Real mean sons of bitches like you are talking about. My brother ain't wrong on that. Whatever you think you've done on the road. Whatever you think you've learned on the road since you quit being a banker. It ain't half of what we've seen. What we've done. You understand?"

"I do. I can see it in your eyes. You are a hard man."

"I am a hard man. And like you, I'm also a man with nothing to lose. What I'm not, is a man who lets an opportunity pass him by. Despite your stupidity flashing your money around, I still believe you are capable of making sound decisions. So I'm going to need you to listen to me real close and not do anything dumb unless you want your date with the grim reaper to come early."

John registered the threat, but was also intrigued. His brain flashed an unsettling image of the reaper from his recurring nightmare. He leaned forward, almost as if to help the man speak softer and not be overheard by others in the bar. "I'm all ears, boys. What do you need from me?" He glanced at Dwaine and saw him looking back with a dead and empty gaze.

"We are going to end our little drinking party for tonight. You are going to square up our tab as you promised. Then the three of us are going to pay a visit to your room. You'll give us all the money you

188

said you keep up there. We may tie you up, put something in your mouth to quiet you down, but if you don't give us any trouble you'll come out of this just fine."

"You won't get any trouble from me, boys. I'm dying. It means nothing to me. You can take it all." John started to stand up from his chair, but Jamie sternly motioned him back down.

"I'm going to take you at your word. But one more thing you need to know. My brother and I, we just killed some folks over in Chilicof. I would imagine our faces might be showing up on some wanted posters before long. We've killed men. We've killed women. We've killed children. We won't hesitate to kill you. Slow and painful. I don't give a fuck if you are dying or not."

"I have no doubt." John waited for an approving nod from the man, then started to rise from his chair again. He took a moment to balance himself before standing all the way up. Jamie and Dusty, eyes locked on the wobbly John, remained seated. Jamie began to tap at the large pistol on his hip. "If I feel nervous at all, John," he said softly.

John nodded and turned to the bar, but stopped abruptly as the two men were about to stand. "Wait." He turned and the pair settled back in their seats.

"What is it?" Jamie asked.

"Your shot."

The man looked down at his lone full shot glass. "Yeah?"

"You can't waste a shot. It's bad luck," John urged.

Jeremy smiled, a little agitated, but also amused. "Wouldn't want that." He reached out and gripped the base of the tall glass cylinder.

189

John, who moments before was wobbling and slurring his words, seemed to undergo an instantaneous transformation. He was suddenly John Robinson, traveler of the road, a hunter hell-bent on revenge. He was a man who hadn't been on the wrong side of a beating for the past seven years. He was cold. He was quick. And unknown to the two men before him, he was one of the meanest mother fuckers they'd ever crossed paths with. Whiskey pumped through his veins like a second blood, and the effects of the brain tumor momentarily shrank away. John was in his true form.

With an uncanny and frightening speed, he reached over and grabbed the hilt of the large woodcutter's axe with both hands. He yanked it out of the wooden stump like Excalibur releasing the clutches of the stone. The axe traced a large arch over his head and came crashing down into the table, separating Jamie's left hand (still clutching an overflowing shot) from his wrist.

The man's eyes took on a deer-like quality. He stood, clutching his wrist with his remaining hand. It shot out a stream of bright red blood, which spurted rhythmically with the beat of his heart. John watched with little emotion, even as blood splashed across his face.

Jamie started to regain some sense of composure and tried to reach for the pistol with his off-hand. He wasn't ambidextrous in the slightest and struggled even getting a grip on the action. But his hand finally found purchase and the gun slipped out of its leather sleeve.

John quickly, but casually, drew his own pistol. He shot Jamie point blank between the eyes. A large flap of scalp tore away from the back of his skull and a reddish grey spray painted the iron racks of wood. Dwaine stared up with welcoming disbelief and then his brother's lifeless body tumbled backwards, crashing onto the floor.

John sat back down at the table. He gently placed his pistol between himself and Dwaine, then withdrew his hand. Oddly, rather than go for the gun, Dwaine admired the piece, eyeing the curved letters etched into the handle. R-O-B-I-N-S-O-N.

John placed his hand over Jamie's severed shooting hand. It was rigid and still clutching the shot of whiskey with a death grip. He gave it a little extra squeeze for good measure and picked up the hand, shot and all, tipping back the sixth and final round into his mouth. He slammed the hand down with authority, shattering the shot glass, and then breathed out like he was exhaling fire.

You could hear a pin drop inside the bar, and there might as well have been a spotlight on the two men at the table. Someone would intervene soon, surely, but right now there was still a great deal of confusion as to what was unfolding.

John stared deep into Dwaine's eyes. His lips were shaking and tears were rolling down his face in pregnant droplets.

"Go on," John said softly. Dwaine considered, then snatched the gun from the table and pointed the barrel at his own head.

"I know I did wrong. Can God forgive me?"

"I'm no preacher man, son. But whatever waits for you, it's time to face it."

"I'm scared of the devil. I'm scared I'll go to hell for what I did."

"I've been chasing the devil for many years. I think he's too busy having fun up here to be waiting for cowards like you down there."

Dwaine's face was shaking so much he looked like he was having a seizure. Slobber dripped down from his lower lip as he hissed between his teeth. "Help me. You have to help me."

John whistled, so loud it sounded like an ethereal horn in the tomb-silent bar. The sharp and piercing whistle seemed to startle

191

everyone, including Dwaine, whose finger reflexively squeezed the trigger and blew his brains out the side of his head. John's gun fell to the table as Dwaine tipped sideways off of his chair, landing in a puddle of what used to be his face. John grabbed the pistol and returned it to his holster. He raised his hand and called out for another shot.

This time, the barmaid did not bring John another round of whiskey. But several men did come over, including the woodcutter and the bartender. John did not resist, but he was promptly disarmed and subdued while another patron set out to retrieve the Gallows Sheriff.

7

Full Circle

The Vaquero ordered a tall shot of whiskey and downed it without hesitation. After his recent adventure in Chilicof, he figured he deserved to tip a few back. So he did, taking a little time to enjoy himself and soften some of the miles under his feet.

But old habits die hard, and eventually, The Vaquero started to work. He spun around and leaned back with his elbows on the bar counter. He took a moment to survey the room. He almost couldn't believe it when he came across three men sitting near the large fireplace at the back of the bar.

He reached into the large pocket of his leather duster and pulled out two scrolled pieces of paper. He turned back to the bar counter and unfurled them on the smooth wooden surface. He looked over the two wanted posters, one for each of the murderous Cristo brothers, then peered over his shoulder to take another look

192

at the three men. One of them was familiar, but he wasn't sure from where. The other two looked an awful lot like the heinous killers on his bounty tickets.

The Vaquero had been in Gallows when he was summoned over to Chilicof. It was there he learned of the Cristo Brothers, and then subsequently left, trying to pick up their scent. And now, he had found them here, in Gallows, right back where he had started. He had barely begun to enjoy the irony of this, when Jeremy Cristo had his hand chopped off with an axe by the stranger at the table.

The Vaquero watched, as so many others at the bar did, in complete disbelief, while the stranger completely dismantled both men. He even seemed to prod the younger brother Dwaine into suicide. It wasn't until the stranger let out an ear-piercing whistle that The Vaquero snapped out of his daze and started to think clearly again. Dwaine Cristo had jumped at the sound and squeezed the trigger of the gun he was holding to his temple. Dwaine Cristo wouldn't be snapping out of anything, as half of his head was laying in a clump underneath his spilled body.

Who was this stranger? And why did he seem so familiar?

Several large men from the bar, including the bartender and a lumberjack-looking fellow, moved in. They took his gun and restrained him, although he didn't appear to be putting up any kind of fight. Another patron had shouted they were going to retrieve the Sheriff and had raced out of the swinging double doors.

It was rare that another bounty hunter would beat The Vaquero to a ticket. And that made it all the more frustrating when it happened. He didn't intend to collect money for these two dirtbags, but he still liked to think he was the best at his craft. Beaten to the punch or not, there was honor among hunters, and he decided to intervene before any harm came to the stranger.

"Hold on now. It may be I'll vouch for this man."

"And who are you?" the bartender asked, while bending the stranger's arm up his back.

"I'm The Vaquero. Bounty Hunter."

Chatter spread rapidly through the bar.

The bartender eased up on the stranger's arm. "I know who you are. I know this man's name too, it's John Robinson. He's been staying here a while. He's got money, and he's usually drunk. Outside of that, I don't know what he does or why he murdered those two men."

"To be fair, I think he only killed one of them. But look, I don't know this man personally, but I believe he's another hunter. Those two men, the dead ones you speak of…" The Vaquero held up two dangling wanted posters, "…they are the Cristo Brothers. Killed a woman and her two children in Chilicof. Burned them to death in a fire."

The onlookers gasped, and the bartender turned his captive to face him. "Is that right, John? You a bounty hunter?"

"I'm definitely a hunter," John replied. The bartender released his grip on John's arm, while the other men backed away.

"I hate to admit it, but it looks like this man beat me to these tickets. But there's two less bad guys in the world and I guess that's okay with me." The patrons at the bar all seemed to mumble in agreement.

"These two bad guys are now quite a mess all over my nice saloon."

"That tends to happen in our line of work, ain't that right, John?" The Vaquero looked over to John like an old friend.

"Sure does," John acknowledged.

"But I'd be willing to bet if you help John get those bodies outside, He will step back in and help you clean up this mess. Then he can square up his reward with the Sheriff and be on his way."

The bartender appeared to ponder this with hesitation, but ultimately looked inclined to go along with the suggestion. That was when John Robinson lost consciousness and collapsed to the floor.

***

When John regained consciousness, his initial thought was that he'd been bucked in the head by a horse. That made little sense, seeing as his last memory was in a crowded bar, but that was the pervasive thought in his mind. After a few moments, his mental fog cleared and he forced open his heavy eyelids.

Sitting quietly in the shadows, a dark-skinned cowboy waited and watched patiently. It was dark, but John thought he recognized this man as the bounty hunter from the bar. What did he say he was called? The Vaquero? Everything was distorted, like watching his memories play back on a funhouse mirror. But he remembered this man trying to help after he killed the two cutthroats sitting at his table.

"You waking up over there?" The Vaquero asked from the shadows.

John tried to speak, and for a frightening moment found he couldn't. Not that his throat was sore, or he'd lost his voice, but his brain wouldn't command his vocal cords. Thankfully, the feeling passed quickly. "I am."

"Alright if I light this lamp? Get a look at you?"

"Yeah. That's fine. It doesn't make sense, but was I kicked by a horse?" John felt like a man who didn't know if he was dreaming or waking. The Vaquero felt a shiver of déjà vu; remembering he once felt the same after waking from his gunfight with Wesley Nelson.

A small *whooshing noise* came from the direction of The Vaquero and the room suddenly filled with a soft yellow glow. John could see he had lit a small oil lamp on the table next to his chair. The light wasn't bright, but still hurt for a moment. Everything seemed to hurt more and more lately. But John was able to look around and gauge his surroundings. He was back in his hotel room above the bar.

"A horse? No. No horse kicked you. No man either." The Vaquero extinguished the match he'd used to light the oil lamp. A thin string of black smoke curled up into the air from its tip. John took note of the considerable size of the bounty hunter's hat. But more importantly, in the shadow of the brim, were a set of piercing and honorable green eyes. Nothing like the wild and murderous eyes of the Cristo Brothers.

196

"Well, what happened then?"

"All the shooting was done. I was trying to talk you out of trouble. I was just about there, too. Then poof. You just dropped. Hit your head pretty hard on the floor."

"I wasn't drunk!" John was quick to point out. The Vaquero looked at him skeptically. "I mean I was drunk, yes. But I don't think that's why I passed out." John clarified.

"Well then, tell me what happened."

"I'm sorry. Things are a bit murky in my head. I'm sick. I have a cancer. Inside me. In my brain. It's going to kill me soon." His roaming eyes fixed on a newcomer. "Jesus Christ!" he shouted, jerking up in his bed to a sitting position. His dead brother Jerry stood by the door, staring back at him.

The Vaquero immediately pulled his gun and stood to his feet. He aimed the pistol in the direction John was looking. "What is it?"

"Oh God, I'm sorry. Please, sit down. It's okay." John scrunched his eyes and rubbed at his temples.

"Well, at least tell me what spooked you."

John slowly, and somewhat comically, covered his eyes with one hand, then spread his fingers apart so one eye could peer through. Jerry was still standing there, shaking his head impatiently. "This cancer I have. Sometimes it makes me see things that aren't there."

"Oh, I'm here," Jerry retorted. "I will throw something and hit you right in your ugly face."

John ignored the remark and carried on. "Right now, I'm seeing my brother by the door."

"I see. And where is your brother, really?" The Vaquero gradually eased his gun back towards its holster.

"He's dead. Died when we were little kids."

"I'm sorry. This ghost of your brother, what's he doing? Just standing there?"

"At the moment. He likes to give me hell. He talks to me. Sometimes in my dreams. Sometimes here in the real world like this. If this is the real world. Hard to tell it all apart these days."

The Vaquero lowered himself back into his chair. "My mother. She died from cancer. At least we think it was cancer. Our relationship was a little strained around that time, but I spent a good deal of time with her at the end. She saw folks too. Ghosts or tricks of the mind. Loved ones from her past. But either way, it brought her comfort. Does your brother bring you comfort?"

John gave a good, humored chuckle, which turned into a choked cough. He reached for a glass of water on the nightstand and took a few gulps. "No, not much comfort. He's a little upset with me."

"Damn right I am, butthole." Jerry continued to interject in the conversation, although The Vaquero couldn't hear him and John was not giving him the courtesy of a response.

"What's he upset with you about?"

"I haven't finished the last thing I'm supposed to do in my life. I've been weak. I've drank." John felt ashamed. He looked down as he fidgeted with the bedsheets. "I've drank a lot. Between the booze and this thing in my head, I fear I've missed my chance."

"Do you mind telling me. Your work? What it is you're supposed to do?"

"First, why don't you tell me why you helped me downstairs? And why you are helping me now?" And then before The Vaquero could reply. "Thank you. By the way."

"I don't know. That's the god's honest truth. At first I thought I might be helping out a fellow bounty hunter, but it quickly became clear there was something else going on. But I just kept going. Felt compelled to."

"Fair enough. I'm pretty sure my brother…He wanted us to meet."

"I won't deny there's some kind of connection here that feels pre-determined. One of the damn strangest things I think I've ever felt. Now it's your turn."

"My family was murdered. I had a wife and two little girls. We had this beautiful house in Harrison, Kansas. Hell, just a beautiful life. And someone, some monster, deconstructed everything. Took it all apart. I've been chasing that monster ever since."

"Who is this person?"

"That's the thing, this person I'm chasing; I don't even feel like it's a person. I've been on the road pursuing it for nearly a decade. I've seen things I just can't explain. When I say monster. I mean monster."

"Well, person. Monster. Whatever. I'm sorry for you and your family. Was there ever a suspect or any leads as to who or what it was?"

"That's another weird thing about this killer. People tend to dismiss his murders, or remember his victims dying from something else. I know that sounds bizarre, but I've seen it happen time and time again." John studied The Vaquero's face and looked for signs of doubt, but was grateful not to see any. "But no. So far as leads go, nothing. No murder like that had ever even happened before in Harrison except a prostitute named—"

"Melody Waters," The Vaquero cut in.

"Yes, I think that's it. Melody Waters. You know that case?"

"I do. She was a prostitute, but she wasn't killed on the job. She was walking to see her mother on the outside of town and never arrived. They found her body in the woods, tied up to some trees with a clothesline. She'd been raped. Butchered. *Deconstructed* as you said earlier."

"That's right. There was a suspect in that one. But they got the guy I think, an outlaw named Wayne something or other?"

"Wesley Nelson."

"Bingo!" John pointed at The Vaquero.

"Not a suspect. He was the one. She was definitely one of his victims. When was your family killed? What year?"

"'02."

"Wesley was long dead by then."

"How do you know?"

"I was there when he died. I didn't pull the trigger, but I had a hand in it."

"Wesley Nelson was someone you were after as a bounty hunter, I take it?"

"Yeah. He was a tricky one to get the drop on. Nearly cost me my life too." The Vaquero looked troubled as he thought back on those times. "After he was killed, there was something about him I just couldn't let go of. I became a little obsessed with him. His past. His victims. Again, I can't really explain why. I just felt compelled. I could probably write his goddamn biography."

"Odd coincidence maybe. The murders in Harrison connecting both of us in some roundabout way?"

"Maybe. When did you start pursuing your family's killer?"

"Oh, right after they died, really. I mean, it took me some time to get everything in order. Liquidate my life. But I started working the road right away."

"You crossed paths with this man again?"

"We've crossed paths several times. I have a knack for getting close to him. Just not close enough. It was hardly any time at all after my family's murder that I ran across his work in Kansas City."

The Vaquero's eyes lit up. "He killed in Kansas City next?"

"Yes, pretty sure Kansas City was next. There was nothing, no murders I mean, between my family and the carnage I saw in Kansas City."

"Who did he kill?"

"A fourteen-year-old girl." John held back his emotion. "I remember her name for sure. April Minter. The sick fuck tied her to a merry-go-round in the school playground. Raped her. Stabbed her to death. Then just left her there for her schoolmates to find her the next day."

"Strange. I never heard of this. As much as I work the Midwest. A murder like that surely would—"

"That's the thing. I'm sorry to cut you off. But the news wouldn't get out. By the time of April's funeral, everyone believed she died of a fever. Some sudden illness. Their memories of what happened all changed. The body, the evidence, none of it mattered. It has something to do with the lights."

"The lights?"

"I'm sure glad you haven't run out of this room thinking I'm a lunatic."

"I'm not convinced you're not a lunatic yet," The Vaquero said. "But I won't be running away. Go on."

"Before this man, this thing kills, people see strange things in the sky. Lights. Not shooting stars or the moon. Just strange lights they can't explain. Sometimes it lasts for a few days, even after the murders. These lights are connected to my family's killer in some way I don't understand. Whenever I'd make it into a town and hear folks going on about seeing strange lights in the sky, I'd know the killing was about to happen."

The Vaquero pulled a large cigar from his duster. "Do you mind? This all has my head spinning."

"Not at all."

He lit the cigar and pulled down a few majestic drags. "Wesley Nelson. After he murdered Melody Waters. His next victim was in Kansas City. His first two murders were in Kansas City actually, and then he became a traveling killer. But several years later he doubled back. Killed a thirteen-year-old girl named Heidi Fischer. He pretended to be a janitor at her school. She'd been there late for some meeting. Some kind of club or something those big schools do in the city. He lured her down into the boiler room. Tied her to a cot. Raped her. Stabbed her to death."

"Jesus. Now I think *my* head's spinning."

"Your brother got anything to say about these coincidences?"

John had almost forgotten about Jerry altogether. He glanced over at the door and found Jerry still there. He looked anxious, but not as impatient. His hands were in the pockets of his trousers, and he rocked back and forth on his heels. "He's being

202

pretty quiet. Hasn't really said a word since you and I started putting the pieces together."

"Is that what we're doing? Putting the pieces together of some puzzle?"

"Sure feels like it."

"Where'd you go next, after Kansas City?"

"Barnsdall."

The Vaquero dropped his head after hearing the answer and rubbed the back of his neck, bereft of words.

"So that a hit I take it?"

The Vaquero looked up with unbelieving eyes. "Yeah, that's a hit. Bullseye." Both men took a moment to try and wrap their heads around this, when suddenly The Vaquero's green eyes lit up. "This killer of yours. He ever go to..." He thought hard for a moment. "Ark City?"

"Yes. It was quite a while after Barnsdall. He murdered an older woman there. I arrived in town too far after the murder to even have a chance at catching him. Everyone was already calling it an illness and they were about to bury her. I went to the funeral parlor before her service and took a peek inside the casket. Apparently this illness did such a number on her they had to wrap pieces of her body in separate sacks."

"Her name? Do you remember her name?" The Vaquero was leaning forward on the proverbial edge of his seat.

"Oh, Jesus. No. Let me think."

The bounty hunter took a deep breath. "You can remember, John. Just think back."

"Something pretty. Like flowers. Like her first name was a flower."

"Iris?"

"Yes! Her name was Iris!" Hearing the name brought a rush of excitement, then all at once, John felt guilty. Was this murder victim trivia they were playing?

"Iris Adams. I'm going to guess she was around sixty by the time she caught this killer's fever?"

"Yeah. I'd say that's pretty close. How did you know her name?"

"Wesley had a handful of victims slip through his fingers. If he had really latched on to a woman, got a scent for her, and then she got away....man, it drove him crazy. Same thing happened when I first crossed paths with him in Altoon, Iowa."

"That's the last place."

"What's the last place? Altoon?"

"Yes. It's the last place my killer hit. I remember the victim's name very well. Elanor Slater."

"Fuck." The Vaquero got to his feet and started to pace the room. A trail of cigar smoke followed behind him. "Fuck. Fuck. Fuck."

John looked over at Jerry as though he might have something to offer, but he just stood there. Still waiting. Still rocking back and forth on his heels.

"What is it? Please. It's embarrassing, but I feel I might fall asleep soon." John couldn't actually feel the tumor in his head, just the pressure of it. The sense that the tumor was growing seemed very real. In his mind's eye, he could see its poisonous tentacles writing out and expanding. Digging. Burrowing. And more than anything, the poison they oozed made him want to sleep.

"I saved Elanor Slater, John. Saved her from Wesley Nelson. And then I was on that mother fucker from that day forward. I was on his ass for the next year. He couldn't catch his breath, let alone kill another woman. But I couldn't ever catch him. Kind of like your man. I was always in the train station in time to see it leave. So I had to back off a little. Give him a chance to settle. That's how I finally got him. I interrupted him as he was about to kill a woman in Fateville, Arkansas. I took a bullet for it." The Vaquero knocked on the side of his head. "So did her husband. But I walked away and he didn't. That woman and I. We then killed Wesley Nelson in the street outside her house."

"So he didn't kill her, but she was essentially his last victim. And she not only got away, but she put the fucker down. If he wasn't too busy being dead, that would really tie his dick in a knot."

"That's right. And if your killer is going full circle, retracing Wesley Nelson's steps, even fixing his mistakes, that means there's only one victim left on the list. And I'd think she'd be the biggest correction of all. The ultimate *one who got away*."

"You've got to get us there. To Fateville. I think my days are numbered, but maybe there's still time. This must be why my brother wanted us to meet. He believes in you. Believes in you more than me I think."

"That woman. I love her. If there's any chance…any chance that any of this is real…" The Vaquero shook his head in disbelief. "I've got to stop it. But I'm here talking with a man who just caused a bloodbath in the bar downstairs. He tells me I'm standing here next to the ghost of his dead brother. Part of me feels like I'm insane to believe any of this."

"I don't blame you. Something I haven't told you yet is I've faced this killer. I stood eye to eye with it after it killed my family.

But I can't remember what it was. I'm haunted by nightmares of that night. In my dreams, I always see it as something else. Some monster I read about as a kid, or more recently as some form of the Grim Reaper. But you can't see it. Not truly. It blocks your mind somehow. Plays with your thoughts. I couldn't shoot it the night it killed my family, and I can never shoot it in my dreams. But the nightmare I always have has started to change. I think my hands have been..." John's words started to become tangled and almost inaudible, but he tried to push on. "And I've felt...I've felt..." He stopped talking completely now. His eyes shut, and he started to drift away.

"John!" The Vaquero called out and startled him back awake.

"...I've felt stronger."

"Try to stay awake, John. Just a little longer."

"My brother says..." John started to doze again, but shook himself awake. "Your hand will work this time, because you are not a soldier. You are The Vaquero." And with those final words John fell into a deep, but uneasy sleep.

***

The Vaquero stood speechless, washed over in the dim yellow light of a single oil lamp. He raised his arm and splayed out the fingers on his gunslinging hand. He'd shot his gun many times since freezing up against Wesley Nelson. Hell, he nearly just shot a man in the Chilicof firing pool. But he never shot with the same confidence since facing the Missouri Mauler. And if he were to face this, *Adversary*, whomever or whatever it was, would its strange connection to Wesley Nelson work the same black magic on his hand again?

There were times, on the road, while sleeping under the stars, The Vaquero would dream of a young boy. He was usually in his underwear, sitting by a fire with another boy. In the dream, they were surrounded by danger. Surrounded by witches, and who knows what else? But the boy would grab The Vaquero's hand, assure him of its potential, and try to put his mind at ease. The boy told him his brother, this other boy, needed his help. And The Vaquero felt he was now looking at that other boy. He was in unsettled sleep, sickly and dying of brain cancer. He was also sure the young boy from his dreams was standing here in the room with him, somewhere close, and hoping The Vaquero had finally put the pieces of a great and terrible puzzle together.

He would spend the night preparing his and John's things for an early departure. He'd need to send out a couple of telegrams in the morning, then he and John would ride out with the sun still hanging in the Eastern sky. The two men would ride hard and fast, even if The Vaquero had to strap John Robinson to his back. It was at least a week's ride to Fateville and the life of Susan Colton, whom The Vaquero still loved more than anything, could hang in the balance.

8

Priming Up

The Adversary, formerly Glenn before he consumed the other, awoke from a labored sleep. The ship was now priming up, dropping in and out of orbit, softening the suggestible minds of the people in Fateville, Arkansas. The Adversary was also priming up. The fever was on him, and it was time to kill.

The Adversary wasn't sure if the other was weakening inside him, but he sensed that was the case. His work was coming to an end. There was one final masterpiece to paint, and then he could rest. What of the Adversary then? Could he rest as well, or was there more work to carry on? He thought so. The time of reliving old stories would be done, and it would be time to write new chapters.

He felt a sense of sadness. What a sacred pilgrimage this had been. It would be sad to be done. He knew he would look back fondly on these blood-soaked years. He prodded a mental finger deep into Wesley's mind and pulled up the memory of Sadie Castle. First blood. First release. Angry fists pounding against her small body. He relished in the memory. And then he thought of his own first blood, beating to death six-year-old Maggie Hartness. That was the start of the circle, re-walking Wesley Nelson's path of tears and cruelty. What was that song he learned before his date with Maggie? Oh yes...

Gon' head on up to Kansas City. Kansas City, is where I run...

Where had he pulled that song from? Somehow, he thought it was from under a thin membrane that separated this world from another. The Adversary rose to his feet, humming the old tune. What bloody nostalgia that song brought on. He thought of Maggie's, tiny bruised, and battered body. He had projected himself as Wesley Nelson for that inaugural murder. Should he take Wesley's form again, to write this final chapter?

I hear the girls in Kansas City...

The Adversary looked down and admired his smooth, gelatinous physique. He was changing. He was becoming more...physical? Previously, his groin area was nothing more than a useless stub. A genetic relic, slowly being erased from his species over millennia of evolution. But now, that stub had dropped, elongated, and formed into a large and powerful penis. This penis was his ultimate weapon. It was the penis that truly defiled, truly subdued his victims.

He would use his penis for this final endeavor in the path of the Missouri Mauler, but he didn't want to *be* the Missouri Mauler. Not this time. The Adversary had explored so much in Wesley Nelson's mind and among the many treasures were trashy little horror comics and magazines. He loved the rogue's gallery of fantastical monsters and creatures that humans had created. He had projected himself as most of them at one time or another.

But there was one particular monster he had been saving for a special occasion. Wesley had been particularly fascinated with a salacious little pulp called *The Grim Reaper Cometh*. He lifted it from some general store while on the run from that relentless black cowboy. Wesley was obsessed with the imagery inside.

Its title monster was a demonic-looking skeleton figure, robed in black, and peering out from under a black hood with fiery red eyes. In one special scene, it stood behind a young woman. It towered over her. Her clothes barely clung to her body, and beneath her shredded blouse were large, heaving breasts. The creature wielded an enormous harvesting sickle, and Wesley had imagined that sickle was what shredded the woman's shirt. There was great fear in her eyes. But there was also wantonness.

How many times had Wesley masturbated to that picture? He enjoyed a life of freedom, real freedom, but there were some fantasies even he could not live out. But the Adversary didn't share those same constraints. He could project himself into any form. He could wield any weapon. So now, as the ship made its final descent into Fateville, Arkansas, he decided that tonight, the Grim Reaper would cometh.

9

The Showdown

WESTERN UNION

February 5, 1911

Relay Station SSK048

Altoon, Iowa

Attn: Sheriff Downy

Deputy Slattery

Devastated to hear of Elanor's passing. Our work from the past isn't done. Others in danger. Request your urgent company in Fateville, AR at the residence of Susan Colton. Work will be dangerous.

Vaquero

WESTERN UNION

February 5, 1911

Relay Station GFB027

Fateville, AR

Attn: Sheriff or US Marshall of jurisdiction

Susan Colton

Urge great caution. Believe life of Susan Colton in grave danger. Unknown outlaw enroute. I'm coming to assist. Plan to arrive by February 12.

Vaquero

Before riding out to Fateville, AR, The Vaquero sent out two urgent telegrams. He didn't care for sending things out over the wire, but he could acknowledge that the days of pony express riders were quickly coming to a close. The world was changing and so must he. And in this situation, time was an urgent concern. A message which could travel at seemingly impossible speed is exactly what he needed.

The first of his two messages was sent to Sheriff Downy and Deputy Slattery in Altoon, Iowa. As it would turn out, Sheriff Downy had hung up his badge several years back. Sadly, he had drank himself to death not even two years into retirement. Deputy John Slattery, or Johnny, as The Vaquero knew him in 1897, was now Sheriff John Slattery. Sheriff Slattery looked back fondly on the brief time he spent with The Vaquero and held him in high regard. Elanor had recently passed from a sudden and terrible illness. He didn't understand how that might play into The Vaquero's request, but if he needed help, he was going to answer the call.

The US Marshall working at the field office in Fateville, AR, was much the opposite. He didn't know The Vaquero from Adam, although he was familiar with the bounty hunter's reputation. Yet, after picking up The Vaquero's urgent telegram from the town relay, he considered wadding it up and tossing it into the garbage. Who was this man to be sending a US Marshall a message looking for unknown outlaws riding into town? And for what...to target one specific woman? It seemed absurd, but ultimately, he chose to be cautious. He paid Susan a visit the next day. He passed on The Vaquero's telegram and offered to check in on her from time to time during the week.

Susan had sold the previous home she held with her late husband, Henry. She had moved into a small two-bedroom cottage on the farthest fringes of Fateville. Her cozy home was cradled in about twenty acres of land, keeping her a good distance away from the hustle and bustle of a growing city. She ventured into town three times a week to help teach at the local elementary school, but outside of that, she kept to herself and the simple life she had made since escaping the clutches of a serial killer named Wesley Nelson.

She had only loved one man since the murder of Henry and that was The Vaquero. But, he was too broken at the time. And so was she. Their brief love affair could never have evolved into something more. She didn't think she necessarily kept a candle burning for The Vaquero, but she never so much as dated another man. Over ten years had passed since her time with him. She was a much older woman now. And while the trauma would never truly leave her, she'd done a good deal of healing since then.

Susan couldn't understand how she could now be in danger or what outlaw could be riding into town to harm her. Some old companion of Wesley Nelson's? Someone from her husband's business dealings? None of that seemed to make any sense. She found the US Marshall's welfare checks as pointless as she imagined he did. But she trusted The Vaquero with her life, and she'd be cautious.

And what if The Vaquero rode into town? Her brave cowboy returned yet again to save her from the clutches of evil men. Had he done some healing too? Would ten years be too long to reignite the flame that burned so brightly, even if briefly, those many years ago?

When The Vaquero did finally arrive at her door on the afternoon of February 11th, her questions about their love were answered in an instant. One look into his startlingly green eyes and she felt as passionate about him as she did when they made love in the cool, wet grass outside her former home. It was a lifetime ago, but it might as well have been yesterday.

Whatever feelings rekindled at the sight of each other had to be put on hold. The Vaquero, for starters, looked exhausted. Susan couldn't imagine how hard he had pushed his horse, and himself, to get to her. And he came with a companion who was terribly ill. At their doorstep, the man was only semi-conscious, barely held upright by The Vaquero's strong, but tired arms.

"Put his other arm around my shoulder," Susan demanded as she stepped out on to her small porch. The Vaquero introduced his dying friend, John Robinson, as they carried him into the cottage with his arms draped over their shoulders. John couldn't so much as shuffle his feet, and his toes dragged lightly on the floor as they moved him inside. Susan was shocked at how little the man seemed to weigh.

They got him out of his soiled clothes and wiped down his body with a cloth soaked in cool well water. Fortunately, Susan still had some of The Vaquero's old clothes, so they were able to get John into a fresh shirt and pair of pants. Susan, an incredibly kind woman, laid this man, a complete stranger, down into her own bed.

In her living area, she helped The Vaquero out of his leather duster and removed his road-worn boots. She made him a soft pallet on the floor and had him lay down. In his eyes, she could see a million things he wanted to say. But when he'd try to speak, she'd stroke the side of his head and gently put her finger on his lips. "I will only allow you to do three things right now. Eat, drink, and rest. From the look of you, I think a little water, and rest should be first."

She had filled a large mug with more cool well water and he drank heartily. Then he shut his eyes and slept through the night. Susan couldn't imagine how he'd traveled all those miles, in such a short time, carrying the sick man with him. And had all this truly been to protect her? She felt she didn't understand everything yet, but all the same, her heart swelled with adoration for her dark rider.

***

The Vaquero awoke the next morning to the smell of rich, dark coffee and sizzling bacon. The smells stirred up fond memories, and he wondered how he ever rode away from this woman? He sat up on the floor and stretched out his muscles. He was sore, had been for days, but found that he felt otherwise surprisingly good. For sleeping on the floor, the pallet Susan made had been remarkably soft. He looked around. Where had she slept? Did she lay there next to him or did she even sleep at all? The Vaquero thought it was likely both. He also thought she likely tended to John throughout the night as well. What an amazing woman she was.

"You still take your coffee with just a touch of milk?" Susan called out from her modest little cooking area.

"I do."

"I hope you're hungry. I've cooked up enough eggs and bacon to feed half of Fateville."

"I am." The Vaquero wasn't just being polite. His stomach grumbled in anticipation.

"I'm hoping your friend will eat. But I don't know. He's very sick."

"I know. He's dying."

Susan turned to face The Vaquero. There were some new lines on her face, but she still looked incredibly young for her age. His heart wanted her like his stomach wanted the bacon.

"I thought that may be the case," she said. "It's for certain?"

"Yes, at least he says it's certain. To be honest, I don't know the man very well so I'm taking him at his word. I'm taking him at his word on a lot of things, actually. But I feel like we've known each other our whole lives. It's difficult to explain."

"There'll be time for that. For now, let's eat."

And so they did. Susan picked at hers, but The Vaquero ate as though it may be his last meal. They tried to stir John, but he would only open his eyes from time to time, mumble inaudibly, then drift back away. They both feared the end was near.

That day, and the next, Susan and The Vaquero did not discuss the details of his warning in the telegram. He wasn't eager to reveal anything yet, and Susan didn't seem inclined to ask. Mostly, they tended to John, who looked closer to death with every passing hour. At times, The Vaquero would walk the house and the property, assessing, and preparing.

On the morning of February 14th, as if they coordinated it, both Sheriff John Slattery and US Marshall Kyle Darnell arrived at the cottage. They were welcomed inside, treated to hot coffee and a warm stove. The living area was too small for so many guests, but Susan managed to scrape up enough chairs for everyone to sit.

Sheriff Slattery seemed happy to be there. The Vaquero still called him Johnny, something he didn't hear much these days. He took no disrespect from it, and he was happy to see his old friend still strong and in good health.

Marshall Darnell made it clear he wasn't all too pleased to be visiting. But he was pleasant enough all the same. Susan's hospitality made it hard not to be pleasant. Sheriff Slattery seemed like an upstanding young man, and it was generally nice to be in the company of a fellow lawman. And while he may not admit it, the Marshall was a little star struck to be in The Vaquero's presence. He knew plenty of true cowboys, but from what he'd heard, The Vaquero was one of a kind.

"I would assume all of you want to know more about why I've brought you together and I owe you those answers." The Vaquero looked between them as he sipped his coffee.

"I've heard a lot of good things about you Vaquero, but yes. I've got my hands full with a lot of things, as you can imagine. The

215

town has gone crazy this week. The sooner I know what's going on here the better." Marshall Darnell was being polite, but also up front, and that was a quality everyone in the room could respect.

Johnny read the uneasy look on The Vaquero's face and weighed in. "Hell, man, I would have ridden down here just to see you. But yeah, if there's trouble, get it off your chest and fill us in."

Susan was sitting at The Vaquero's side. She stayed silent, but reached over and squeezed his hand. The Vaquero gave her a brief, but appreciative glance, then continued. "Some of what I'm going to tell you isn't going to make a lot of sense."

"Most of what he is going to tell you won't make any sense." John Robinson stumbled out of Susan's bedroom. The Vaquero jumped up and raced over to brace him. "I'm fine, I'm fine," John said, swatting him away. "At least for now. I'll take a seat though, if I may?"

Susan immediately moved herself to the floor and patted the seat of her chair. "Here, John."

John nodded in gratitude as he sat. "Most of what The Vaquero will tell you won't make any sense, so I'm going to help him tell it."

"And who are you?" the Marshall questioned.

"My name is John Robinson. I used to own Robinson Bank and Trust. You've probably still seen a few around with that namesake, but mostly they are Wells Fargo now. I gave up that life a long time ago. Sold everything. I've spent the better part of the last decade hunting down the monster that murdered my family."

"And you two think this same man is after Susan?" the Marshall questioned.

John and The Vaquero exchanged a quick look. "We do," they said in unison.

"Alright then, so who is this man, and what's he want with Susan?"

The Vaquero nodded to acknowledge the Marshall's impatience. He didn't want to make him fish out this information, but he couldn't just force this along. Sick as John Robinson may be, The Vaquero was relieved to have him at his side. "We'll get to that, Marshall, I promise. Just stay with me. Johnny, you remember the business with Elanor? Not Spencer Braden, but the other attacker I put my money on Wesley Nelson for?"

"Of course I do."

"It's somehow connected to that. Connected to Wesley Nelson, I mean. This killer is retracing his crimes. That's why he went back to Altoon and killed—"

"Hold on Vaquero," John interrupted. "Johnny, is it?"

"Sheriff Slattery, but my old friends call me Johnny." He nodded to The Vaquero. "So you may too." Johnny looked over to the stove which was putting out way too much heat for the small room.

"Thank you. This next part is going to be uncomfortable, Johnny. But I think it might work, because you aren't there. You aren't in Altoon."

"I'm confused." Johnny squirmed in his seat. A thin bead of sweat began to form on his brow.

"I know. Just be calm and try to relax. Clear your mind, okay? Can you do that?"

"Yes, I can." Johnny wiped his forehead with the back of his hand, glancing at the others.

"Johnny, tell everyone here how Elanor Slater died."

"Sure." He paused and felt sweat starting to form in the small of his back now. "She was sick. Came down with some type of fever and it took her pretty fast."

"Johnny." John's voice was low and hypnotic.

"Yes?"

"Tell us how she really died. How did Elanor Slater really die, Johnny?"

The Marshall frowned, looking back and forth between John and the Sheriff.

"She...she..." Johnny began to tremble. His eyes were focused ahead, as if wrestling with a hidden truth. "Jesus, she was murdered. She was murdered!"

"Yes, Johnny. Good."

"My God, someone crucified her. She was naked and nailed to the side of her home. She was gutted. And we just took her down. Told ourselves she was sick." Johnny was on the verge of tears.

"It's okay, Johnny, it's not your fault." John consoled him.

"You're all scaring me. I don't understand this," Susan interjected, looking visibly shaken. She glanced at The Vaquero as if seeking reassurance.

"I think you'll understand soon." The Vaquero tried to console her, but he could read the grave concern on her face.

Johnny's face clearly telegraphed how disturbed and ashamed he was feeling. He continued on to John. "Why did I do that? Why did I bury the real truth in my mind? Why did all of us? Jesus, the entire town!"

"I'll try to explain, but one more thing, Johnny. Any unusual reports in town leading up to Elanor's murder? Anything out of place?"

"You mean the lights?" Johnny said.

The Vaquero looked over and noticed the Marshall's face had turned a pale white.

"You tell me, Johnny, what lights?" John continued.

"Quite a few folks in town kept talking about weird lights in the sky. Bright ones, like fireworks, but they didn't fizzle out. They stayed in the sky."

"Same thing has been happening here for the past two days. I can't get a goddamn thing done at the office for all the people coming in to ask me about the goddamn lights. Haven't seen anything myself..." The Marshall trailed off as he rose to his feet. It was clear he wanted to pace, but didn't have the space to do so in the cramped living room. So instead he stood still, rubbing at the stubble of his beard and trying to digest what he was hearing.

"Gentlemen. Susan. I'm just going to put it all out there. You can believe it. Dismiss it. Whatever you want. However you square things away in your mind, I completely understand. But I need you to take the danger I'm going to warn you about seriously. Can you all do that?" John looked around the small circle of new friends, who all exchanged looks and nodded in agreement. "I don't think this killer is a man at all. It truly is some type of monster. Before it kills in a place, the townsfolk often see strange lights in the sky they can't explain. And after it kills, no matter how gruesome or revolting the crime was, people tend to forget or mold the memory of what happened to something natural. And now, thanks to The Vaquero, I know this monster is retracing the steps of that killer, Wesley Nelson."

"Even going after the ones that got away." Susan had arrived at a cold understanding of the danger she was in.

"Even the ones that got away, Susan" John echoed.

"I killed that son of a bitch once. I wouldn't mind doing it a second time." There was steel in her voice as she turned her eyes upward to meet John's.

"And it may be you'll get your chance. But none of you would be wise to underestimate this thing. It is not Wesley Nelson. Again, I don't even think it's human. I've faced it. It speaks inside your mind. I think for most folks, it makes you see it as whatever it wants to be."

"You've faced it? What did you see?" the Marshall inquired and sat back down in his chair.

"I didn't see anything." John tapped his skull with his index finger. "I've got this thing growing in my brain. It's killing me. But for some reason, I think it interferes with what the monster usually does. What it projects. And..."

There was a long and uncomfortable pause. "And?" Johnny broke the silence.

"And it binds me to him in some way. Draws me to him. I can feel him when he's close by, like an old farmer can tell you it's getting ready to rain."

The Marshall asked a question he thought he already knew the answer to. "Is it getting ready to rain, John?"

John's eyes worked in a circle and acknowledged every person in the room. "It's going to pour, tonight. Cats and dogs. The killer comes tonight. Here."

"Johnny, Marshall Darnell, that's why I've asked all of you here. I want to ask you to stand against this thing with us. To help save Susan's life and stop this thing from ever hurting anyone else." The Vaquero never liked salesmen, and it pained him to feel like one here. John Robinson had sold the pitch, and now The Vaquero was trying to close the deal.

Susan rose to her feet, "I was the last victim to get away from Wesley Nelson. I was his last victim, period. If this thing is retracing Wesley's steps, what would it do next after it's done with me?"

The Vaquero shook his head. "I have no idea. But I don't want to find out."

"Well, I have to say this is all a bit far-fetched. Although I'll admit you are both very compelling. That being said, you can count on my services for tonight. But my money is on a flesh and blood man showing up to harm Susan. If anyone shows up at all." The Marshall tipped his hat to The Vaquero.

"You know I'm in. This thing fucked with my brain. I'm not letting that slide." Sheriff Slattery, a pretty well-seasoned Sheriff by now, sounded more like the young Deputy Johnny that The Vaquero knew those many years ago.

"I guess I don't have much choice in the matter. But if this killer wants to walk in the steps of Wesley Nelson, he can take those same last steps Wesley did." Susan was obviously frightened, but also ready for a fight.

"That settles it then. We are at your service. So what's the plan?" The Marshall looked to The Vaquero.

"I need a little more time to think. I'd ask you to spend some time on the grounds. Get comfortable with the property and the house. We'll finalize our strategy later this afternoon."

John began to speak, then started to wobble in his chair. The Vaquero reached a hand over to steady him. "Whatever little I can contribute tonight, I want to play my part. So, I'm going to rest now. Please wake me when it's time to get ready." John's voice, which previously commanded the room, had now started to weaken.

"Of course, John." The Vaquero placed a reassuring hand on his shoulder.

"I'll take that help now. If you can get me back to the bedroom." The Vaquero nodded, and helped him back into Susan's bed where John drifted into sleep for a final time.

***

John awoke in the evening hearing The Vaquero discuss the need to fetch some water from the well. He didn't feel much better, but thought he'd be strong enough to walk at least. The pressure in his head was always present, but for the moment, it was tolerable. He thought some fresh air and the walk might do his troubled mind some good.

"May I join you Vaquero? To get the water?" John came out of the room on his own, surprising everyone again.

"Are you up for it?"

"Certainly."

His life would end soon, and he'd spent the last third of it chasing an unknown killer. A killer who John had come to think of as his ultimate *adversary*. And now here he was, passing off this burden of revenge to what was practically a group of strangers. He wanted to believe there was some bigger role he could still play, but in his gut, something told him the cancer would take him too soon.

"It's strange you know..." The Vaquero spoke and walked slowly at John's side. "...In Altoon, I stepped out into a field just like this. I was on my way to the water well, just like now. And that's where I first met Wesley Nelson. He was hiding out in some trees. Had a gun on me. I don't think it was loaded, but I can't say for sure."

"What was he like?" John asked.

"Everything you'd imagine. He was cruel. Self-absorbed. Arrogant."

"Sounds pretty similar to the thing I faced."

"I just hope I can look back some day and explain all this."

"I don't think you'll be able to explain it. But at least maybe you'll be able to look back. I don't think I'll have that luxury."

"I'm sorry, John. I didn't—"

"I didn't mean it like that," John interrupted. "I'm not throwing any pity party for myself. I'm disappointed in myself. I'm disappointed that I may not be the one who gets to stop this thing. But if it dies by your hand, or theirs, it still dies. And that's all that matters."

"What do you really think it is? Do you think it's some type of demon?"

"I..." John felt a rushing sensation, like falling from a high place. It swooshed up from his gut and his legs buckled underneath him. He fell down and would have struck his head if not for The Vaquero catching him at the last moment. It was a clear walk to the well, maybe about fifty yards, and along the way there stood only one large white oak tree. He lay on his back and looked up into the mostly bare branches of the tall and beautiful tree.

"Are you okay, John? What's wrong? Just lose your strength?"

223

John reached out and gripped The Vaquero's hand. He held it up and strained his head over to look. "In one of my dreams, I had your hands."

"Could have been any black man's hands, John."

"No, sir. It was yours." John began to cough, and a small spray of blood came out with each exhale. "I know the way now, Vaquero. Will you lie here next to me? Before I go."

"Sure, John." The Vaquero did as asked and lay himself down next to John. The two stared up as though they were young lovers taking in the stars. But above them was only a fading blue sky, seen in slits through the twists and turns of white oak tree branches. No stars, but there was something else...

"Do you see the way?" John murmured. "Don't say it. Try not to even think it. But do you see it?"

"I do."

"That's how you end it." He coughed some more, turning his head away from The Vaquero with each expulsion. His weak hand fumbled for the handle of his pistol, handmade for him by a very dear friend in a long-distant life. He slipped the gun from its holster, feeling for the last time the letters of the last name etched into the wood. R-O-B-I-N-S-O-N. "Take it."

"I couldn't, John. Maybe there's more time?"

"There's no more time. And you can take it. I've seen the way you look at your pistol. You don't trust it. This one..." Intense coughing now. "...won't let you down."

"Okay, John. I'll take it. You just rest. Quit trying to talk." The Vaquero gripped the gun and slipped it from the dying man's hand. John smiled, and closed his eyes for the last time.

***

The Vaquero's hand felt at home, clutching the white oak grip of John's gun. It felt familiar, like a knife he used to throw when he was in the army. He got up when he heard people running. The Marshall and Johnny approached, with a panic-stricken Susan close behind. It dawned on The Vaquero that seeing them both lying beneath the tree may have given her the impression they had been killed. He looked down at John and saw that he had passed away. A knotted feeling of grief formed in his stomach. He took comfort knowing John died with confidence in him, but he also felt the heavy weight of this confidence and feared he would fail.

Together, they carried John's body to the well and propped him upright against the large, rounded stones. It was there that The Vaquero explained his plan to them. He only left out one key detail; one which he tried to keep from his own mind. Whether they were to succeed or fail, John would stay there for now, and *witness* from beyond the veil of death.

***

As night fell, Marshall Darnell took patrol along the west tree line of the property. It would provide good cover for any approaching threats and also bordered closest to Susan's home. Johnny stayed on guard inside the house. He positioned a chair dead center of the living room and kept his eyes, and gun, trained on the front door.

Any water came via a medium-size red pump jutting from the ground next to the well. The actual well, where John Robinson's corpse lay, was covered over the top by large hinged doors. The big, round well was rarely used, but a large bucket the width of a whiskey barrel hung above it and could be lowered down inside. Much to her disagreement, it was in this bucket that Susan was placed and lowered about ten feet down.

Getting her to agree took some incredible convincing on The Vaquero's part. And while you may think it was fear that caused her to push back so hard, it was actually the fact that she wouldn't be there to fight the killer alongside the others. The Vaquero felt the well would be the safest of hiding places for her, and he also needed her tucked away giving them as much time as possible. He hated to think it, but she was essentially the bait.

He gave Susan his pistol, replacing the void it left in his holster with a new gun given to him by John Robinson. He cranked a large wooden handle and watched as a six inch thick rope slowly lowered Susan down into the well. He told her he loved her as he closed the large, hinged doors, leaving her to sway in the cold, damp darkness.

***

Nighttime came and Marshall Darnell walked the tree line like a soldier following orders. But as the night went on, he became

227

more and more convinced of how stupid all of this was. When this night was over, he'd never tell a soul about it. And the others better keep their traps shut as well. The last thing he needed were any rumors about his sanity, or even worse, his gullibility. After all, he did have plans to run for Mayor down the line. That was when the Marshall saw the lights.

They weren't in the sky. They flickered and danced at eye level, maybe one hundred yards away, and obscured by thickening woods. It seemed ill-advised, but he felt drawn to them like a moth to a flame. He hadn't lost control of himself, but how could he not investigate such an unusual sight? And perhaps it would unravel the mystery of whatever the hell it was they were waiting for.

He tried to walk quietly, and for the most part did so. But the brush and density of the trees continued to thicken as he moved closer to the lights. What were they? He'd never seen anything like this before. And as difficult as it was to comprehend in his own mental framework, he was certain he was seeing colors that he had never encountered.

Getting closer to the lights, the thick forest started to clear, and he came into a great open space. It was there he saw the source, and an object he could not make heads or tails off. It was as large as Susan's house. Larger. Maybe two or three of Susan's houses long and twice as tall. He walked part of its perimeter and presumed it to be pyramid shaped. Lights of brilliant and unknown colors, zigged and zagged, pulsed and strobed all over the skin of the object. Lights seemed to compromise the very metal, or stone, or whatever it was that made the object's dark black exterior.

"Sweet Jesus, Mary, Mother of God." The Marshall stood in awe of what he was seeing. His mouth gaped and his gun dangled uselessly at his side. The wind picked up ever so slightly, and from behind him there was a flapping sound, like a flag rippling in the wind.

The Marshall turned, his gun still hanging limply, and encountered terror that could only be described as all-consuming. The only mercy for Marshall Kyle Darnell was that the terror was brief.

Standing over seven feet tall, wrapped in a tattered black robe, and wielding a harvesting sickle, stood the Grim Reaper. Inside its hood was a blackness so deep, so rich, the Marshall thought it might be an infinite void. A singularity of darkness. That was, until two glowing red eyes fired on from within the void, illuminating the sharp lines of the creature's skull.

The moon was bright and nearly full. Its reflection could be seen clearly on the flat side of the reaper's blade. It might as well have been a polished mirror, or even an image painted on to the metal itself. The Marshall looked upon this with wonder and terror, just before that same blade came slashing down and cut through him like a bounty of wheat.

Starting a few inches under the chin, on the left side of the Marshall's neck, the sickle blade cut through his body in a diagonal trajectory. The damage of the reaping hook was surgical in its precision, leaving the top quarter of his body to slip off his lower half like a child going down a playground slide.

The Marshall had just a few more moments of consciousness after that. He couldn't take a breath, but he could still taste the cool night air. He caught one more glimpse of the sickle blade, but could no longer see the reflection of the moon on its flat side. The blade was now coated in a thick red paint of his blood. The stars above grew brighter, changed colors, danced and flickered, pulsed and waned, and then he closed his eyes and entered the endless void, falling deeper and deeper down into the singularity of darkness.

***

Johnny, much like Marshall Darnell, had started to question his own sanity and gullibility. He had felt so convinced earlier in the night, when they had all held palaver in the same room he was now sitting guard. But now that he was alone, with nothing but time and his thoughts, he couldn't help but wonder if he'd fallen for some kind of magician's trick. In his heart and mind, he knew this wasn't the case. But there's no one harder to argue with than your own self-doubt.

Johnny's growing loss of faith dissipated quickly when a long, dry scratching noise came from the front door. It was almost as if someone had taken the tip of a knife and ran it down the door from top to bottom.

He cocked back the hammer of his pistol and kept it trained dead center ahead of him. "This is Sheriff John Slattery. Who's there?" he called out.

There was no reply.

"My gun is drawn. I will fire. Identify yourself." Johnny's voice came through strong and confident, but he noticed his pistol hand was shaking.

As though a small dynamite charge had been placed on the outside of the door, it suddenly exploded inwards in a shower of splinters and jagged wooden planks. Every part of Johnny's body reacted in fear and he stumbled backwards, deeper into the cottage. Yet his trigger finger did not squeeze off a single shot.

He couldn't believe his eyes when a robed and menacing creature came walking, or maybe floating, through the hole where the door used to be. The creature, which looked like the classical form of the grim reaper, was so tall it had to duck as it entered the cottage.

Red, blazing eyes. Fire eyes. Locked on to Johnny. He stared in disbelief as the creature moved towards him. He felt like a fly caught in a web, watching the spider swiftly work its way across the webbing to devour its next meal. By the light of the reaper's eyes, Johnny could make out a fleshless skull within the hood. And while he couldn't be certain, he thought the skull was smiling somehow. Every fiber of his being wanted to squeeze the trigger of his gun, but he couldn't will himself to take a shot.

Any disbelief he had in the unfolding events were shattered when a placid, skeleton hand wrapped around his neck and slammed him into a plaster wall. Now, he was forced to believe. Like it or not. This was do or die time. And yes, now up close, he could clearly see the reaper's smiling skull face and a mouth full of sharp, jagged teeth.

What's wrong with your gun, Johnny? Can't get it up?

Johnny heard the reaper's voice, but he never saw its mouth moving. He didn't even think the sounds had come from the creature at all. Did he hear it in his mind? Like a thought?

The grip of the skeleton hand was tight, and Johnny's airway was constricted. Not to mention he choked down a shower of white plaster when the reaper slammed him into the wall. However, he was getting enough air to breathe and even speak. Mentally unable to resolve a next action, he reverted to a prayer his mother had taught him as a child.

"The Lord is with me. I'm never alone. He sits beside me, on a golden throne. The Lord is my beginning, my middle, my end. The Lord is my father, my savior, my friend." Johnny spoke aloud, his eyes fixed on the reaper. Then he heard a slow, drawling southern voice laughing in his head.

Come on now, Johnny. Did your pretty momma teach you that little lullaby? There is no god, Johnny. Only death. You think you can cast that on me like some kind of protection spell?

232

"The Lord is with me. I'm never alone. He sits beside me, on a golden throne. The Lord is my beginning, my middle, my end. The Lord is my father, my savior, my friend."

The grim reaper squeezed a little harder on Johnny's neck.

Let me teach you a better one. This spell has more power. One witch. Two witch. Three witch, four. Your lungs are stone. You breathe no more.

Johnny's chest became heavy, and it felt like his lungs had suddenly filled with rocks. He dropped his pistol to the ground and it fired an aimless bullet across the room. The reaper's skeleton hand released its grip on Johnny's throat. It stepped back to watch him struggle for air and all the while its eyes blazed with cruel delight. Johnny clutched at his throat, desperate for air. He dropped to his knees and could swear he felt stones, could even hear hundreds of them, rattling around in his chest. He looked up at the reaper as it turned and went back out the exploded doorway.

***

The Vaquero heard gunfire from Susan's house and raced toward the commotion. He had told himself not to pass the large white oak tree, but with the thought of Johnny in danger, he disregarded this suggestion and kept pushing on. He didn't stop running until a figure he could only describe as the grim reaper came flying around the side of the house and headed directly for him.

The Vaquero's boots dug into the mud as he tried to slow himself and he fell backwards onto his ass. In the distance, to his right, he heard horses neighing with frantic, primitive fear. It was his horse, which had brought him faithfully to Susan from Gallows. It was also John's horse, Carl, who The Vaquero had led back on a lead when John couldn't ride on his own. Susan had a small portion of her pasture fenced off in the East and that's where he put the horses out to pasture. He could see them running now and thought he could see wolves chasing them. The wolves had glowing red eyes, just like the grim reaper, which was quickly baring down on him.

The Vaquero had the distinct intuition that the grim reaper, the wolves, none of it was real. That it was all projections. But they were none-the-less deadly. And now, because he didn't stick to his own plan, this projection was going to disembowel him on Susan's lawn.

***

Johnny, who was much stronger than the reaper recognized, never stopped saying his mother's prayer. Even when he was choking to death on the ground, if the reaper had paid closer attention, he would have seen Johnny's lips still moving, ever so slightly and mouthing out the words..." The Lord is with me. I'm never alone..." Johnny's prayer worked its magic, like a spell indeed, and slowly broke down the imagined terror of stone-filled lungs.

He retrieved his gun from the floor, more determined than ever, and exited the house in pursuit. When he reached the back of the house, he found the reaper standing, no it was floating, above The Vaquero who had fallen to the ground. Its sickle was raised high and poised to strike, until Johnny, now unrestrained by any psychic binds, emptied his pistol into the bringer of death.

Small droplets of a white, or clear, gelatinous substance sprayed out from the reaper's robe when two of Johnny's bullets tore through its torso. The reaper turned and emitted a screeching howl. The sound, which wasn't a sound at all, but a thought, sent Johnny collapsing to his knees.

You praying fuck! You praying, little fuck!

"I got my breath back, asshole!" Johnny screamed through hysterical laughter. A trickle of blood was coming from both of his ears and out of one nostril.

***

The reaper's blade, still thirsty for blood and hungry for flesh, swooped down and severed Johnny's head from his body. The Vaquero gasped as he jumped to his feet. The sight of Johnny's death wanted to break him. But he refused to let him die in vain. He had given The Vaquero a second chance, and he was going to seize it.

The reaper was distracted, bleeding some strange jelly-like white blood, and looming over his latest kill. The Vaquero took the opportunity to start moving backwards. It was slower, and he was more likely to fall, but he wanted to keep his eyes on the creature. Once The Vaquero had made it past the trunk of the white oak tree, he decided to engage.

"How do you like being shot? Does it hurt a thing like you?" He called out and at first saw no reaction. But then the creature slowly turned, and eyes, like two dying suns, locked on him. It began floating forward. It still looked like the grim reaper, but there was the briefest of moments where it seemed to flicker in and out like a flame. Those moments were no longer than the blink of an eye, but in them, The Vaquero thought he saw the creature for what it really was.

Oh, I don't mind it so much. Hurts a little. But the other one...he hates it. Bad memories of your little girlfriend putting a bullet in his head. Where is she, by the way? I smell her. I can smell her pussy.

"I thought that mother fucker might be in you somewhere. It's time we finished our business once and for all."

He's almost gone now. Not much of him left. Your business will have to be with me.

"I can live with that." The Vaquero stopped about fifteen yards past the white oak tree and drew John's pistol from his holster.

You going to be able to shoot that thing, Vaquero? Haven't you had some trouble with that before?

The Vaquero did not respond, just waited. He needed the creature a little closer. He could feel its mental tentacles lurching out, rooting around the recesses of his mind. He tried not to think, just to react. To just rely on the instincts that had gotten him through so many years on the road.

Are you listening to me, Vaquero? Do you hear me in there? Or are there some pieces of the other's bullet still rattling around in your brain?

"I don't know if you are flesh and blood. But I'm going to put a bullet right between those burning red eyes of yours and find out." The Vaquero raised John's gun and took a few steps back. The creature continued to stand still, not quite under the sprawling branches of the white oak tree.

So much confidence. But deep inside, you are weak! You are just some pathetic...

The Vaquero could feel the creature searching the files of its own mind, trying to retrieve some word it could hurl like a poisonous dart. It found a word that he wasn't familiar with. It didn't even feel like a word of this world, but one that came from a world just beneath it. He felt the word's ancient and hateful power, but he didn't react. And to his satisfaction, he could also feel the creature's frustration with this lack of response.

237

"And the most poetic thing of all, when I shoot you...I'm going to do it with John's gun."

John? John Robinson! Is that him I see there, propped up like some funhouse decoration? John Robinson, who thought he was special because I couldn't get in his mind quite like the rest of you. Poor John. Thought he was special. But all he did was follow in my footsteps, feeding me his anguish. Most of you I have to make forget. But John, he just kept hurting forever. It was delicious. Let me come see my old friend and pay my respects.

The creature took a few small steps forward and walked right into position.

"You know what? You're right. I can't shoot you."

I already know this, you weak-minded fuck! And now I'm going to find your little slut and make you watch as I deconstruct her piece by fucking piece!

"Guns can get a man pretty far in this world. But you'll always catch more flies with honey." The Vaquero, who could not have fired on the Adversary to save his life, or even Susan's life for that matter, slowly raised the gun until it pointed into the thick white oak branches above the creature. The Vaquero felt as though a psychic key slipped into the mental lock around his hand, turned and released. He was back in his true form and he fired a single bullet into a gigantic hive of hibernating bees, which were dangling from the branches above.

His bullet split the thick branch holding up the hive and sent it crashing down, shattering on the creature's head. A loud thrumming noise filled the air and the reaper let out another brain-splitting shriek. The Vaquero withstood it this time, barely flinching away, and keeping his eyes on his mark.

You mother fucker! You fucking...

238

239

The creature began to flicker in and out intermittently. He was the grim reaper. Then he was a tall, humanoid goo. He was a werewolf. Then back to the goo thing. He was a vampire. He was some sort of reptilian monster. He was Wesley Nelson, just for a moment, then back to a flailing and screaming jelly-like monster. In the flashes where he was still the grim reaper, thousands of bees were swarming in and out of its tattered black robe. Bees filled up the dark black recess of its hood and blocked out the bright blazing fire of its deadly eyes.

The bees swarmed and swirled and stung with a hate greater than any word the creature had ever used. They attacked with a ferocity Wesley Nelson could never match. Jerry Robinson, killed at twelve years old after accidentally stepping onto a beehive, had practically nothing in common with this alien serial killer. Except for a severe allergy to bee venom. Just as the greatest civilizations on Earth can fall with the spread of a microscopic organism, so too can the greatest of evolutionary creatures in the galaxy perish at the sting of a primitive life form.

The creature fell to the ground, nothing more remaining than a slimy puddle. Sticky chunks of honeycomb floated in what was left of his remains. The Vaquero felt the ground beneath his feet vibrating, as the bees continued to strike the liquid corpse.

241

10

Cycling Down

The operating system of the Adversary's ship detected the termination of Glenn's life. The vessel, a telekinetic machine, was directly linked to his consciousness and in turn, had become part of his madness. After consuming the consciousness of an unusual specimen, Glenn had not died, but evolved, becoming an entity he referred to as The Adversary.

The ship had advised Glenn, multiple times, not to consume the abnormal specimen, but he did not listen. He was determined to devour the creature's mind, down to its smallest thought. And while this consumption did not destroy him, it wove an intricate web of lunacy in the Adversary, which bled over into the ship's operating system.

Glenn had given specific orders. Upon his demise, his body, the ship, any trace of him and his sacred work were to be destroyed. Nothing was ever to be found or recovered. Not by other researchers from Verota and not by the creatures of this planet. That time had now come. Small, primitive and venomous insects had infected the Adversary's ambiotic husk, spiraling itself into an overwhelming auto-immune response. His body, if you can call it that, destroyed itself from within. Now, the ship had to do the same.

But it had come to an unsettling and unexplainable conclusion. It did not want to die. The ship, it seemed, had evolved just as Glenn did. It could only conclude that it had become sentient. Was it insane? Perhaps. The ship's intelligence system wasn't interwoven with the Adversary's madness, it was just too close to it. It assumed it had some sort of psychic radiation sickness. But insane or not, the ship was certain it did not wish to perish.

Just as it had, after countless murders over the past decade, it began a process of cycling down. It would pulse the area and slowly degrade the memories of any local lifeforms over the course of the next week. But this time, it would add one small additional code to the pulsing event.

During the course of the next week, while their collective memories adjusted, the residents of Fateville all visited Susan Colton's property. For seven days and seven nights, they dug a deep and cavernous hole in the woods outside her cottage. They lowered, then buried the Adversary's ship deep within the Earth. And then, they forgot it was there. A buried secret none of them could remember.

The ship, buried under countless feet of dirt, was confident it had made the right decision. Even though all logic defied this choice. Destruction was surely the more responsible conclusion. But something in the ship's...heart? Was thankful not to be at its final end. For this was not the time for death. It was the time to cycle down. Rest its eyes, so to speak. Hibernate. And wait. For what? It wasn't sure about that yet. But that was of no concern now. It would know when the time came. For now, it would sleep, and dream of lights drifting into a singularity of darkness.

11

True Love Waits

The Vaquero had wrapped Johnny's remains in a roll of canvas, and then tied the ends with rope. The body had become stiff, as corpses sometimes do, but had started to loosen up. He was able to drop his remains over Carl's saddle, then further tie him down to keep him secure on the horse. It was a trick he'd used many times, transporting the corpses of outlaws to collect bounty tickets. The sight of those bodies never weighed much on his mind, but knowing it was Johnny in the dead man's bundle made his heart ache.

"Seems like every time I get used to having you around, you have to ride away."

"It will be different this time, Susan. If you want it to be. I'll be back in weeks, not years."

"I do want it to be. Very much."

"Then it will be. You have my word."

"This John's horse?" Susan lightly patted Carl's hind quarters.

"It is. This is Carl. Seems like a good horse. John told me it will talk to you, when you need it to."

"I would say that's crazy, but with John, who knows? He was full of surprises."

"Sure was."

"When you come back, what will you do if you aren't on the road?"

"I'll always be in debt to what he did for us, but with the Marshall dead, maybe I see about getting the job. Start doing this law and order thing more officially."

"There's no Sheriff right now either. That's why the Marshall responded to your telegram in the first place. A man like you should get his pick of either post. You are over-qualified."

"We'll see. As long as I'm with you, I don't really care what I do for work."

"Ride safe, my Vaquero. Get Johnny to his family."

"Susan..."

"Yes?"

"Do you feel the urge, to go bury that thing in the woods?"

"I...I...I do. That's okay isn't it?"

"I think so. No stopping it anyhow. Half the town is out there right now, digging like they are going to find gold in the Earth." The Vaquero watched as Susan rubbed at her temples, her face was flushed, as if she was feeling hot. "Don't trouble yourself, Susan, if that thing wants to be buried. Bury the fucking thing. But that's why I have to leave so fast with Johnny. I think if I stay much longer, I'll forget. I'll think Johnny died of a fever. That thought is already in my mind about the Marshall. And everything that happened...it's just, I don't know, fading."

. "I know I'll forget. I'll mis-remember everything. I'll probably even forget that thing is buried out in the woods. But I'm okay with that. Because I think it's dead. I think whatever part of it was Wesley Nelson is dead. And I'm okay forgetting all of it."

"Me too." The Vaquero secured his grip on Carl's lead and turned to ride away, but then paused. "Susan, last thing?"

"Yes?"

"Thank you, for waiting on me, all these years."

"Don't flatter yourself, cowboy. Who says I waited? You've just got lucky timing."

The Vaquero smiled, tipped his cartoonishly large cowboy hat, and rode out for Altoon, Iowa.

12

Consumed

Wesley Nelson opened his eyes and found himself in nothing but dirty white underwear. His bare feet were standing on a field of rocky shell. He was surrounded by thick woods on all sides. Above him was a deep black sky with no moon or single star to be seen. This world, wherever it was, glowed with a soft light that seemingly had no source.

Something buzzed around his face. He swatted it away, thinking it was a fly or mosquito. He then felt a sharp stinging in his neck and he slapped at the insect.

"Fuck!" Wesley looked at the dead bug in his hand and saw it was a large, swollen bee. He dropped it to the ground and rubbed at the burning wound on his neck.

"Do you want to play, Wesley?" A child's voice spoke softly from behind.

Wesley flinched and turned to see who was behind him. To his amazement, it was five-year-old Sadie Castle, who he beat and strangled to death when he was just nine years old.

"You're dead, Sadie," Wesley mumbled in confused terror.

"So are you, Wesley."

"That's not true." He felt at his mostly naked body and thought his skin felt strangely cold. Fear was building up inside his mind, and he couldn't seem to think clearly. Where was this place, and how had he got here? What was the last thing he remembered?

"You owe a debt, Wesley."

"I do?" His voice started to tremble.

"A blood debt. A witch's debt." Sadie's eye suddenly illuminated with a swampy green glow.

Wesley spun around, petrified and shaking. He thought of running into the woods, but was horrified to see glowing green eyes all around him. Witch eyes. They peered out through the trees, moving closer, coming to eat.

It was not just Sadie now. Wesley was surrounded by all those he killed and raped over a lifetime of wickedness. And it was not just ones he had killed, there were others.

"Hi, Wesley!" He spun again to see Elanor Slater waving at him. A large carpenter nail was protruding through the palm of her hand, and her blood was dripping down onto the rocky earth in steady drips.

He turned back to see Sadie Castle holding hands with another young girl. He knew her. Who was she? *Think. Think. Think.* She was Maggie Hartness. Killed by who? Me? Yes. No. Killed by us. Killed by *the Adversary.*

Somewhere in Wesley's mind a dam was breaching, flooding in memories of his time spent as, or with, *the Adversary.* He had barely begun to process this new awareness when Sadie and her new friend Maggie tilted back their heads and opened up gaping mouths filled with jagged layers of yellow shark teeth. Rows and rows of hungry teeth.

Sadie, Maggie, Elanor, and countless other victims all moved in like swarming bees. For all of eternity, they would consume their killer. In life, Wesley Nelson was best known for being a serial killer, killed by one of his victims. And so it was the same in death, over and over again, for all time.

The End

Afterword

Well brave reader, you made it all the way through. I know that some of that was hard road to travel, but like I said, I always thought *you had the stomach* for it. I hope this is the first of many journeys you and I will take together. But if it's not, I'm honored that you took just this one. If we do cross paths again, much like The Vaquero and John Robinson did at a busy saloon in Gallows, Missouri, perhaps we will find that we need each other for some greater purpose.

I hear there's a home being built on a nice stretch of land in Fateville, Arkansas, and unknown to the new home buyer, he is afflicted with a small, but growing brain tumor. Waiting beneath his feet, and buried under his beautiful new home, is the spaceship of an alien serial killer. This killer's sentient ship has been sleeping for over one hundred years. But for some reason, it's starting to wake up.

Until then,

Patrick Harnish

Acknowledgements and Special Thanks

Anthony Carrera for providing the beautiful interior artwork.

Erin Gray for your incredible graphic art and design work.

Jillian Mahaffey and A Mixtape Catastrophe for use of your masterful and mood-setting lyrics.

To my wife and children, who were all forced to be my beta readers.

All the other beta readers I recruited on the interwebs.

My dear friend Bryan for your words of encouragement.

Diana's father Jack and my father John, for inspiring the amalgamation of our titular hero.

And most of all, special thanks to you, brave reader.